THE THIRD URBAN FARM FRESH ROMANCE

Memories of Mist

First edition, GreenWords Media, 2017

THE THIRD URBAN FARM FRESH ROMANCE

Memories of Mist

VALERIE COMER

GreenWords Media

Dedication

For Diane

Acknowledgments

Thanks so much to my many readers who've asked for the next installment of the Urban Farm Fresh Romance series. I know it's taken a while, but I hope you feel your patience was rewarded!

Thanks to Elizabeth Maddrey, first reader and idea-bouncer. Your help was invaluable as I threaded my way through this volatile story idea! Thanks also to Tina, Rebecca, and Paula for your eagle eyes and great suggestions in the beta reading department. All of your input made this story so much better.

A big thank you to my fabulous editor, Nicole, who sees beyond words, punctuation, and sentence structure to the heart of the story.

I'm also grateful for the Christian Indie Authors Facebook group and my sister bloggers at Inspy Romance. These folks make a difference in my life every single day. I'm thrilled to walk beside them as we tell stories for Jesus!

Thank you to my Facebook friends and followers! We had some lively discussions on the pitfalls of parent-teacher dating, the joys (I use that term lightly) of team-building exercises, and the thrill of seeing our kids take off as readers — and what their first solo chapter books might be. I loved having your ideas and input! Thanks for the collaboration.

I extend my apologies to the Spokane School Board for taking liberties with their school system and morphing it to fit the needs of this story. I took extensive literary license, and I freely admit it.

I am ever thankful for my husband, my hero and champion, who selflessly gives of himself, never hesitating to jump in and protect the ones he loves. He's also a constant advocate for my work, standing behind me 100%. Jim, I can never thank you enough.

To our kids, their spouses, and our four little grandgirls: thanks for your love and support... and for not thinking it's weird for your mom, mom-in-law, and grandmother to be an author. Or, if you think it, you don't mention it in my hearing! I love you all so much, and am thankful for you every single day.

All my love and gratitude goes to Jesus, the ultimate hero, who "demonstrates His own love toward us, in that while we were still sinners, Christ died for us." (Romans 5:8, NKJV) What more could any hero do for us than deliver us before we even knew we needed rescuing?

Books by Valerie Comer

Farm Fresh Romance Novels

Raspberries and Vinegar
Wild Mint Tea
Sweetened with Honey
Dandelions for Dinner
Plum Upside Down
Berry on Top

Arcadia Valley Romance Novels

Sow in Love (Romance Grows in Arcadia Valley)
Sprouts of Love
Rooted in Love
Harvest of Love

Urban Farm Fresh Romance Novels

Promise of Peppermint
Secrets of Sunbeams
Butterflies on Breezes
Memories of Mist
Wishes on Wildflowers

Christmas in Montana Romance Series

More Than a Tiara
Other Than a Halo
Better Than a Crown

Riverbend Romance Novellas

Secretly Yours
Pinky Promise
Sweet Serenade
Team Bride
Merry Kisses

Chapter 1

NO WAY. "A NEW TEACHER?" Adriana Diaz stared at her friend. She'd been looking forward to this meeting with her daughter's second grade teacher, a woman she'd come to respect in the past three years. "What happened to Mrs. Lopez?"

"Her husband got a surprise promotion and transfer to Boston. She notified the school two weeks ago."

How had the grapevine missed her? "So what did we get with such short notice?"

Heather Sund grinned. "A hunk." She elbowed Adriana. "Too bad I'm married."

Adriana sighed. The sting of losing Stephan had lessened over the years. That didn't mean she was on a manhunt the way Heather assumed. Raising two kids alone took all the time and energy she could muster.

"Violet is going to be crushed." Just like her mother. "Sam loved her last year, and I thought this would be a teacher who would *get* her."

Heather laughed. "Desiree was looking forward to second grade with Mrs. Lopez, too, but she met Mr. Sheridan half an hour ago, and she's already decided she's going to marry him someday."

Desiree wasn't Violet. Violet was a challenge, to put it lightly. Adriana dreaded her daughter's teenage years with foreboding as strong as she'd felt the night nearly five years earlier when Stephan had been called out to that fire. Somehow she'd known he wasn't coming home long before the fire chief showed up at her door, hat in hand.

The monitor of Bridgeview Elementary came into the hallway. "Ms. Diaz?"

Heather gave Adriana a nudge. "Is Violet at the playground with Desiree?"

Adriana blinked. "Yes. Would you mind sending her in?"

"My pleasure." Heather leaned closer and waggled her brows. "Call me later. I want to know what you think of our new teacher."

Um, yeah. Like Adriana was going to walk through the door into the second grade classroom and fall in love with her daughter's new teacher in fifteen minutes flat. "Thanks for getting Violet." She turned and entered the space.

A tall man with dark hair and a short beard stood to meet her, a smile on his face. "Ms. Diaz? And... Violet?" He looked behind Adriana. "I'm Mr. Sheridan. Myles."

"Yes, I'm Adriana Diaz. My daughter will be here in a minute." She reached out her hand. "It's nice to meet you, Mr. Sheridan."

Heather was right about the hunk part. The man was awfully good looking, and the smile on his face seemed as genuine as his casual shirt and black jeans, just within the dress code for Bridgeview's teachers. To say nothing of how warm his hand felt in hers.

The hand she was still holding. Adriana pulled back. She didn't have time to waste before her daughter entered. There was no way to know whether Violet would bounce in happily, or skulk in with a snarl.

"So you'll be the second grade teacher this year." *Nice opening line, Adriana. Smooth.* "It's unusual to find a male teacher in the younger grades. What made you choose this age group?"

He blinked. What, he hadn't expected to defend his choice? "I enjoy children. In the past few years I've taught mostly upper elementary, it's true, but I appreciate the innocence of younger ones. They're not as jaded and bored with the whole school thing yet."

Adriana glanced over her shoulder. "You haven't met Violet. No one has called her innocent since she was a baby."

Mr. Sheridan's smile held. "Each child is an individual. What is your daughter passionate about?"

Passionate about obstinacy did not seem to be the appropriate response. "She loves art. And recess."

The man chuckled. "Don't we all love recess? Tell me about your family, Ms. Diaz."

"My husband was a firefighter who died in the line of duty several years ago."

"I'm so sorry to hear that."

"I have two children. My son, Sam, is in third grade, and you'll soon meet Violet. I work from home with two quite different jobs. I'm both a seamstress and a bookkeeper for several small businesses in Bridgeview." She paused. "How about you, Mr. Sheridan? What are you excited about?"

"I... uh, teaching. I love teaching."

"What subjects? What are your after-school hobbies?"

13

"I enjoy cycling and swimming. Skiing when I get a chance. Also, I'm an avid reader. And you, Ms. Diaz?"

The man kept volleying the questions back to her. Probably fair. After all, she wanted him to understand her daughter. Violet was the sum of her experiences thus far, and that included her home life.

Adriana resisted a shudder. She needed to get some better experiences into her daughter, if that was the case. "I love to cook. You'll find Bridgeview residents share an interest in local food. We have several ongoing initiatives, such as a new community garden that will be ready for next spring. We're also in the process of creating a permaculture food forest and, as you know, the Parent Teacher Association has just raised the funds for a greenhouse and fenced garden for the school. How do you plan to take advantage of that space in your teaching?"

He opened and closed his mouth.

She finally had Mr. Sheridan at a loss for words.

"Gardening isn't really my strong suit, and second graders don't require it, thankfully. Ms. Bertoli will ably pick up the children's education in this area in third grade."

"Pardon me?" Adriana took a step closer. "You can't be serious. Mrs. Lopez had the entire school year planned around the greenhouse and school garden. The children are looking forward to it, and so are the parents." She angled her head. "I'm sure the school board made the expectations clear during your interview process, short as it might have been."

"This isn't a private school, and gardening is not a core curriculum, Ms. Di—"

"It's core in Bridgeview."

"The state—"

"We expect our children to learn reading, writing, and

14

arithmetic, of course. But isn't there more to life? Personally, I think there is much more." She needed to get this all said before Violet came in, awkward as it was. "I think a healthy approach to food is vital for everyone, and so do the other members of the PTA. That's why we worked so hard to make this happen, even within the public school system."

"I don't disagree, Ms. Diaz, but the teaching approach may vary." The teacher's smile looked forced. "I have a full year planned without a gardening component. I'm sure you'll understand."

Adriana took a deep breath. "No, I don't. The greenhouse is there for every classroom, and the parents of Bridgeview Elementary School expect it to be used."

Bet he could hardly wait until her fifteen minutes were up and he could meet the next parents. But this wasn't something she was willing to concede. Not after all the fundraising and grant-writing and everything the PTA had gone through. Her daughter needed this type of curriculum now, this year.

"Hi, Mom. Desiree said we have a new teacher. Is this him?"

Adriana turned. Her child stood in the doorway, feet planted and arms crossed as she stared over at the man.

"Mr. Sheridan, my daughter, Violet. Violet, this is Mr. Sheridan."

"How come he's a man? Where's Mrs. Lopez?"

She'd skip the first question. "Mrs. Lopez moved to Boston, so she can't be your teacher, after all."

"Hi, Violet. I'm pleased to meet you. We're going to have a really good school year. Your mom says you like art—"

"Yeah, I like art. But what are we going to do in gar-

15

dening class? I can't wait to grow stuff in the greenhouse."

Mr. Sheridan shot a sideways glance at Adriana. "We won't be having gardening class this year. That will pick up next year, when you're in third grade."

"That's not fair." Violet's chin quivered as her voice rose. "That's Sam's grade. Why can't we have it now in this class?"

Myles Sheridan stared at the belligerent girl with her arms crossed in front of her. *Forgive me, Lord. I know every child is important, and this one is no exception.*

But gardening? The board had mentioned the greenhouse acquisition, of course, but not a single member had balked when he stated that his class wouldn't be making use of it. No one had warned him that the parents of Bridgeview Elementary were this set on the gardening component. Ms. Diaz and her daughter weren't the first to exude frustration.

The expression on both faces in front of him was similar. Not particularly friendly. The mother had been on guard when she first entered, but now her lips were drawn into a tight line and her brown eyes flashed dangerously, not diminishing her natural beauty.

He'd met a mom or two with an agenda in his previous schools. Myles generated a smile for the child. Once she was won over, her mother would back off. "What was your favorite thing about this summer, Violet?"

She shoved dark blond hair off her face. "I went to the rodeo with my grandma and grandpa. There were even kids doing mutton bustin'. That looked like fun, but my grandpa said I couldn't try."

"Mutton busting?" That was a new one. Myles couldn't help glancing at Ms. Diaz.

"Sheep riding, like bull riding for children," the mother clarified. "The one who stays aboard the longest wins."

"I see." He looked back at Violet. "I hope you'll draw me a picture of that event on the first day of school."

The child shrugged. "Maybe."

Myles glanced at the clock on the wall. The next parent and child were likely waiting in the hallway by now. "It's been nice meeting you, Violet. Ms. Diaz. School starts at eight-thirty next Tuesday, right after Labor Day. I look forward to making this your best school year ever." That line seemed to have more of a ring to it when he taught sixth grade.

"Before we go, Mr. Sheridan, I'd like to hear you address some ideas for use of the greenhouse space for your class. This is something the PTA has worked hard to bring to Bridgeview Elementary, and we're not about to let one rogue teacher derail our program."

Rogue? "I hardly think I'm de—"

"Perhaps that was the wrong word, but how would you feel if your child's second grade teacher didn't think reading was important, Mr. Sheridan? Is it okay to take a year or two off? The children can always pick it up later, right?"

"Excuse me, Ms. Diaz. I hardly think this falls in the same category. You are talking about a garden."

"There are adults who do not read, Mr. Sheridan. Some who cannot, and some who can't be bothered. I'm a reader myself, and I read to Violet and her brother every day. But it is possible to function in society with very limited reading ability."

He crossed his arms and leaned against his desk. "Your point?"

"My point is that everyone in America eats every day, whether or not they read. Yes, some are more fortunate than others as to the choices they are offered, but an early introduction to the basics of nutrition is vital in this day of childhood obesity, to say nothing of society's obsession with technology. Learning to grow food hands-on will open as many doors to our children as reading."

She couldn't be serious. School gardening class as an antidote to childhood obesity? As important as reading? He met her unyielding gaze. She was absolutely serious.

"I'll consider it." That was the best he could offer to clear the air and make way for meeting the next family.

She rested her hand on her daughter's shoulder. "I'm sorry the school board didn't make the situation clear, Mr. Sheridan. I look forward to hearing your plans for implementation soon. Feel free to ask if you have any questions about what is age-appropriate."

Uh, not likely. Myles scratched his neck. "I did say I'll contemplate it."

"I'd appreciate that. It's very important to me and the other parents, Mr. Sheridan." She turned to her daughter. "Coming, Violet?"

The child raised her eyebrows at him as her mother guided her through the doorway.

Myles let out a long breath. Fit a greenhouse into his carefully written plans? Face down this mother-daughter pair? The choice was like choosing which way to drown.

Chapter 2

WISH YOU WERE STILL WORKING at the elementary school." Adriana poured a cup of tea for her best friend, Rebekah Roper. It was a lovely afternoon to visit on the back deck. A gentle breeze lifted cool air from the river beyond, riffling through the turning leaves. "Although I totally understand why you're taking a leave of absence."

Rebekah cradled her one-week-old daughter in her arms. "I do miss the kids and the teachers, but yeah. Olivia needs me right now." She picked up the cup and took a sip.

"I know." Adriana could hardly take her eyes off the baby. It seemed forever since Sam or Violet had been that tiny. "I just don't know what to do about Violet's teacher. You heard they hired a man to replace Mrs. Lopez?"

"I've been out of the loop. But a positive male influence should be good for her, I'd think."

"Well, yes, though Sam probably needs it more." Adriana moved two bowls of Apple Brown Betty from the tray to the patio table and reached for Olivia. She couldn't take it any longer. Her arms craved that baby. "May I hold her?"

Rebekah kissed the downy head and passed the infant

over. "I'm not very good at one-handed eating yet. Sometimes it seems all she wants to do is nurse."

"She's still adjusting to life on the outside." Adriana nuzzled the soft cheek. "So sweet. So innocent." Would she and Stephan have had another baby if the fire hadn't claimed him? Violet had just turned two. It was hard to remember any measure of innocence with that one, which brought the new teacher back to mind. "His name is Mr. Sheridan. Myles Sheridan."

Rebekah's spoon paused halfway to her mouth. "The teacher?"

"Yes. Sorry. I'm very disappointed in the board's choice. Mrs. Lopez was as vital a part of getting the greenhouse and school garden in place as anyone in the PTA. Mr. Sheridan isn't the slightest bit interested. He figures Natasha can pick up that part of the children's education in third grade."

"Oh, that's a problem."

Finally someone who saw it her way. "The school board apparently didn't think so." The baby let out a thin wail, and Adriana jiggled the wrapped bundle as she paced her spacious deck. "I wish going to them would help, but it won't. They've already hired him, and the school year's begun."

Rebekah ate quickly, probably counting the seconds until Olivia refused to be satisfied with anything but nursing. Adriana remembered those days all too well. Her kids had been so much easier after weaning, when Stephan could take his turn with them. Man, she hadn't thought about Stephan this much in a day for a while.

"I imagine it was hard to find a new teacher on such short notice. What are Mr. Sheridan's plans for his class, then?"

"I'm not sure. He seems an avid outdoor enthusiast.

Claims to love reading as well."

Rebekah tilted her head. "How old is he?"

"Not sure. Thirty-something, probably? It sounded like he had a few years of teaching under his belt already."

Her friend's brows rose. "Thirty-something?"

Great. Now Rebekah had *that* look in her eye, just like Heather Sund. Adriana swayed with the baby. "I didn't ask him."

"And an outdoor enthusiast? So I'm guessing he must be fit."

"Not that it matters."

Rebekah giggled. "Sure, it does, if he's to be an example to the children."

"We need him to be an example in the gardening department. Rebekah, you know how hard we've worked to get that component set up. To get the funding. Volunteer hours to prepare the site. And now one out of seven teachers is not planning to participate? That's means fourteen percent of our student body won't garden. Completely unacceptable."

"To say nothing of it being Violet's class."

"Exactly. She's been looking forward to it so much. As much as a child like her can look forward to school at all. She's devastated."

"I'm sure you'll do your best to support the new teacher even though you don't agree with him. A good example will go a long way to helping Violet adjust."

Adriana narrowed her eyes. "I'll support him if he reworks his curriculum."

"And that's the message you want to send to your children?"

Silence reigned on the deck for a long moment while

Adriana stared at her friend. The chickens squabbled over a choice bug in their temporary pen on one of the garden beds beyond. Rebekah's words struck home, but that couldn't mean she should just give up without a fight. Did it? She shook her head and shifted Olivia in her arms.

The baby turned her face, mouth open in search of food as she whimpered.

Adriana brushed her lips over the soft cheek. Olivia turned toward the touch then began to cry in earnest.

Rebekah held out her arms. "I'll feed her." She adjusted her clothing and snuggled the baby against her breast. "Tell me more about Mr. Sheridan."

"There's not much to tell. We butted heads straight off with the garden issue."

"What outdoorsy things does he like to do?"

"He said something about cycling and swimming."

"Thirty-something and buff. Cute?"

That would be one word to describe him. Adriana glared at her friend. "If you like men with a beard."

"Beards can be quite attractive if kept trimmed. Does it look good on him?"

"What does it matter?"

Rebekah looked up and held Adriana's gaze. "I'm concerned for you. You're such a dear friend to me, and I only want you to open yourself up to the thought of allowing a man into your life. A good man. A Christian man."

"I have no idea if he's a Christian or not." Maybe she'd been a bit too pushy, though. What if he found out she was a believer, and her attitude turned him away from faith? "Anyway, you know I'm not looking to get married again."

"So you've said. Why not?"

"Because." Adriana's arms felt empty without the

newborn. She wrapped them around her middle. "No one can replace Stephan."

"I'm sorry I never got to meet your husband. He must have been pretty much perfect."

Was Rebekah making fun of her? It was hard to tell. Rebekah and Wade had moved to Spokane — separately — two years back, reignited an old romance, and were now happily married new parents. What could Rebekah possibly understand about the trauma of losing her husband? Not that Adriana would wish the experience on anyone.

"No man is flawless, Adriana. Even Wade or Stephan." Rebekah tucked the blanket tighter around the baby as a cool breeze swirled up from the river beyond the deck. "Also including Mr. Sheridan."

The men shouldn't be mentioned in the same context, though her friend was right. Not everything about Stephan had been perfect. They'd had their share of arguments and adjustments. It was easier to remember only the good times. But, if she'd developed a selective memory that marriage equaled only sweetness, shouldn't she be open to experiencing it again? Obviously she didn't think the same thing could happen a second time.

The reality was, they'd had a few problems. A good chunk of that had been Adriana's own fault, for sure. She knew where Violet got her strong will from. "No, Stephan wasn't perfect. I don't have him on some kind of pedestal, no matter what you think."

"Then consider dating again?" Rebekah's eyes met hers. "I don't mean the new teacher, necessarily... unless, of course, he turns out to be a Christian and you're mutually attracted. But just have an open attitude toward the fact that God might bring someone into your life?"

The problem with married friends was that they thought everyone else needed the same thing to be fulfilled. Adriana was past that. Hadn't she built a good life for herself and the kids? Hadn't she adjusted to being a single parent over nearly five years alone? "I don't need anyone. And besides, can you just imagine the awkwardness of dating my child's teacher? No, thanks."

"So you're saying that if romance was a gift God wanted to give you, you'd tell Him you knew better?"

How had Rebekah gotten to know her well enough in the past two years to cut so close to her heart?

Myles looked around the two-bedroom basement suite. It hadn't been updated since the seventies by the looks of the fake-wood-paneled walls and the harvest gold appliances. At least they weren't avocado. Could this become his new home?

A child yelled in the fenced backyard, and Francesca Amato turned toward the steps leading up to the carport. "Take your time and poke in the corners. I'll be right back." The sound of her footsteps faded.

The commute in from Spokane Valley wasn't that long. He could keep his apartment there. It was bigger. Airier. But Dakota Jorgenson, the fifth grade teacher who'd decided to pursue him last September, had moved into the building over the summer. She wouldn't take no for an answer, sort of like that one mother he'd met today in the parent-teacher interviews.

He shook his head and crossed the space to look out the

living room window into a fenced backyard with several raised beds loaded with tomatoes and green beans.

Gardens again. Myles turned away. He didn't want to think about Ms. Diaz's challenge. He already knew he was going to cave in, because who needed that much conflict? But it chafed, and when was he going to find the time, especially if he was moving?

And he had to move. Living in the same building as Dakota when he had the option of somewhere else was a recipe for disaster. He'd switched jobs, switched cities, to get away from her. Switching apartments as well was a no-brainer.

Was this the one? He turned and surveyed the space again, hands behind his back. The L-shaped kitchen looked decent enough for his simple needs, so long as the appliances worked. A few built-in bookshelves and space for his desk with cable and internet provided. An extra bedroom for his home gym. The rent was decent.

Footsteps sounded on the concrete stairs outside, and Fran swept back in, a toddler with a smudged face in her arms and a little girl by the hand. "Say hello to Mr. Sheridan, Tieri. Mr. Sheridan, this is Tieri. She's in kindergarten this year and she just loves Miss Wendell. Don't you, sweetheart?"

The little girl nodded, squinting up at him.

"Pleased to meet you, Tieri." Myles squatted and shook her hand.

"And this is Luca. He just turned two in July. I promise sound doesn't travel too much through the floor, Mr. Sheridan."

Myles offered a smile. What was the definition of *too much?* But there didn't seem to be much else available within Bridgeview, and the idea of cycling or walking to work was growing on him, to say nothing of leaving Dakota behind. "You know, I think I'll take it, if you can hold it for October first. I'll need to give my notice at my other apartment." Thankfully he had a couple of days yet before the end of August to turn it in.

"Sure, we can do that, or you can put two hundred down and move in any time, with full rent starting in October. No need to try to juggle moving in a single day that's not even on a weekend."

"Really? That would work for you?" Myles hadn't dealt with a real person in a while. Property management companies running multiple buildings didn't offer deals or personal touches.

"Sure, why not? My husband and I talked it over last night and agreed." Tires sounded on gravel beyond the open doorway behind her and a car engine cut out. "There's Tad now. Go get Papa, Tieri."

The little girl scampered up the steps and came back a moment later with a man about Myles's age in tow. The man stretched out his hand. "Tad Amato. You're Myles Sheridan, the new teacher?"

Myles gave it a firm shake. "Yes. Pleased to meet you."

The toddler leaned from his mother's arms and was scooped into his father's. Tad nuzzled the little boy's neck, and the child giggled with delight.

Something inside Myles shifted. Tad Amato couldn't be much older than him, if at all. He had a wife, two children, and a real home. Myles had a career, terrific exercise equipment, and a lot of books.

Dakota Jorgenson was definitely not the right woman for him to build a family with, but it was time Myles began contemplating settling down. The woman he fell in love with would be sweet and mild-mannered. She'd be several years younger than him — under thirty, for sure — with no encumbrances. She'd be a whole lot different than Adriana Diaz.

Now, where had that thought even come from?

Chapter 3

ADRIANA WAITED IN THE SCHOOL corridor as the children from Mr. Sheridan's classroom rushed past.

"Mom? What are you doing here?" Violet stopped in the doorway, frowning and seeming unaware of the jostling around her.

"Hi, sweetie. I need to talk to your teacher for a minute. Wait in the playground, okay?"

Her friend Sabrina grabbed Violet's arm. "Come on!"

Violet narrowed her gaze at her mom before turning away. "Okay." But she didn't sound convinced.

Interrupting Violet's routine was always a little risky. Not that the child stuck to them very well herself. It was fine if she was the one to change things up, but someone else? Oh, boy. Mr. Sheridan had probably already discovered that. With a wry grin, Adriana entered the classroom.

Myles — no, Mr. Sheridan. She needed to keep that distance. The man crouched, listening intently to Sky Romero's tale. The small boy from a broken home desperately needed positive attention, and it looked like his new teacher was up for the task.

Mr. Sheridan's eyes crinkled at the corners as he spoke to Sky in words too quiet for Adriana to pick out. She took in the sight of him for a moment. His beard wouldn't be allowed at the fire department, but why would he care if a face piece would seal or not? He was a teacher, not a firefighter. Certainly a safer career than the one that'd taken Stephan. Myles's brown hair was trimmed neatly, but still much longer than Stephan's buzz cut. Really, there weren't many ways the two men were alike.

What was curious was that the comparison even roamed through her head.

The little boy giggled and turned toward the door.

Myles — Mr. Sheridan — glanced up and saw her waiting. The smile faded from his face as he rose, and his eyes grew wary. "Good afternoon, Ms. Diaz."

"Good afternoon, Mr. Sheridan."

"What can I do for you today? If it's about the bug collection, Violet said—"

She waved a hand. "No, nothing about bugs." Though her daughter hadn't mentioned a project. Hmm.

He waited.

Drat, the man was going to make her come out and say it. "I've been wondering how plans for incorporating the greenhouse and garden are coming along."

"I haven't had a lot of time to make decisions of that nature."

"It's been eight days."

"Eight days in which I've accepted a new position, found a new rental, given my notice, and begun packing." He snapped his fingers. "Oh, and spent four of those days actually teaching."

"A new position?" Dare she hope he was moving on again? Adriana shoved the slight surge of hope down where it belonged. How would the school board fill a vacancy during the school year? Violet wouldn't deal well with a stream of substitute teachers.

Myles's jaw firmed. "This one, Ms. Diaz." His finger circled and pointed at the floor between them. "This is my new job. Teaching second grade at Bridgeview Elementary."

"Right." How had she lost control of the conversation? "We're very happy to have you here."

His eyebrows rose.

Yeah, she didn't even believe it herself. He disconcerted her. Him with those blue eyes piercing her thoughts. It took a lot to gain the trust of one of the Romero kids. Sky had actually giggled. Adriana had known the family for a decade — well before the little guy's birth — including the three years since the parents' ugly breakup.

Myles Sheridan was not an evil man. He simply wasn't aware of how important the school greenhouse project was to the entire community. Had anyone else even talked to him about it? Or were the other parents just glad the board had found a replacement for Mrs. Lopez? Too bad there wasn't a Santoro child in this classroom. Marietta, the matriarch of the large Italian clan that made up a good percentage of Bridgeview's population, wouldn't let Mr. Sheridan get away with this. She'd be a good ally.

Adriana startled and blinked. She was still staring into Myles Sheridan's blue eyes. His eyebrows were arched above them, and his mouth twitched... with repressed laughter? "I'm sorry. I was, um, lost in thought."

"I noticed."

"You said you're moving. Into Spokane?" Did she even know where he'd come from?

"Yes. Right into Bridgeview, actually. I've given notice on my apartment in Spokane Valley."

There weren't many rentals in the neighborhood. But hadn't Fran and Tad's renter moved to Seattle? Fran wouldn't have... "Oh, whereabouts?"

"Basement suite a few blocks over. Close enough to walk or bike to the school."

Adriana's heart sank. "The Amatos."

"Yes, that's them. I should have realized you'd know them."

"Everyone knows everyone in Bridgeview. Fran is one of my closest friends." Or had been. Although it wasn't fair to blame her and Tad for taking rent money from Myles Sheridan. They needed the income. She couldn't know how big a problem this was for Adriana. For the school.

"They seem like a very nice family."

"They are." How had they veered off into this subject? Time was ticking. Violet would only be happy at the playground until her friends' parents picked up their kids. But how could Adriana pull the conversation back to the greenhouse?

"Violet's adjusting well, in case you were wondering. She's very bright."

Adriana blinked. "Yes, she is. She cooperates when she thinks it is her idea."

Mr. Sheridan's mouth twitched in the midst of that beard. Did she imagine a twinkle in his eyes? The gleam disappeared so quickly she couldn't be sure. How dare the man laugh at her? Assume Violet was stubborn because her mother was?

31

"If there's nothing else, Ms. Diaz, I need to tidy the classroom and head home to pack."

She stiffened her spine. "Go ahead, Mr. Sheridan. Don't let me keep you." She turned and marched out the door, down the corridor, and out to the playground. *Don't let me keep you*. What a dumb thing to say. As though she had him and was releasing him. No matter what Rebekah said, she wasn't looking for romance. Especially not with Myles Sheridan.

For all he'd claimed he had places to go and things to do, Myles stood at the classroom window and watched Adriana Diaz push her daughter on the high swing while chatting with two other mothers. Adriana tipped her head back and laughed, her brown hair swinging nearly to her waist. She was quite pretty, really. At least when she wasn't trying to make a point with her daughter's teacher.

A rustle sounded behind him, and Myles turned.

Natasha Bertoli smiled as she came toward him. "Hey, there. Just checking how the first few days at BES have treated you."

He could relax. This third grade teacher wasn't Dakota. She was married, for one thing. Hopefully happily. "Going well, so far. Thanks."

Natasha strolled nearer and looked out the expansive window. "You've got a better view than I do. Across the corridor, it's just straight up the hill, brambles and all."

It *was* a good view. Even if it was hard to look past the women and children in the playground and between the houses across the street all the way to the river far below.

The other teacher's gaze followed his. "Have you met Adriana Diaz? You've got Violet this year, don't you? I've got Sam."

"Yes, we've met. She's something else."

Natasha chuckled. "She's a great mom, really involved in her kids' lives. She'd do just about anything for the school."

He turned toward the other teacher. "She's after me about the garden and greenhouse project."

"Oh, I bet she would be. She was president of the PTA for two years — taking some time off now, I hear — and the whole team worked very hard to get the school board to approve their proposal. To say nothing of all the fundraising they did, the grants written. All that."

"Do you think I should change my plans?" The words were barely out before Myles regretted them. He wasn't a newbie teacher. He was perfectly capable of creating his own path and following through.

Natasha shrugged. "Up to you, of course. She isn't going to relent, and many of the other parents will back her, although she's the most vocal."

"Parents don't run the classroom. Or at least they shouldn't. It's the teachers who are trained to make the best decisions for the classrooms."

"I hear you. But, on the other hand, it's not just her. It's the whole parent-teacher association, and Bridgeview's parents are very involved."

"The school board didn't seem concerned about the curriculum."

"They needed a replacement to fill the position, and they didn't have a lot of time in which to find someone. You had the experience necessary." Natasha spread her hands. "From their point of view, it was a slam dunk. How it works out on a more practical level is up to the school."

"And the parents." Man, he hated being herded.

Natasha nodded. "I'm sure I don't need to tell you that teachers don't work in a vacuum. Maybe in some inner-city schools they do. Having engaged, caring parents is far more a blessing than a curse."

"So long as they remember who the professionals are. Those who're trained to deliver the best educational experience. Years of college." Too bad people weren't required to take courses before they could become parents.

"Of course."

Outside, the swing slowed to a stop, and Violet jumped off. Sabrina and her mother strolled out of the schoolyard, arm in arm. A boy came around the corner walking a dog nearly as tall as himself on a leash.

"That's Sam," Natasha offered.

"That is a humungous dog."

"Duke is a gentle giant." The other teacher grinned.

Violet wrapped her arms around the dog's neck and kissed him on the nose. Didn't she know about germs? About the places dogs' noses sniffed? Adriana, her two children, and the huge canine turned left at the school gate.

Myles shook himself. Did he want to keep fighting with that woman? He hated conflict, but something about her made him feel like digging his heels in and staying obstinate. Adriana had a point, as his fellow teacher reminded him. If he held firm, it was going to be a long school year, and he'd likely find himself at odds with more than one parent. So far, no one else had caught on.

"Bianca left her research materials with me, if you're interested in having a look."

He glanced down at Natasha. "The teacher I replaced? Why would she do that?"

"She was as passionate about the project as the PTA, quite frankly. Her husband's transfer to Boston nearly caused a separation, if not a divorce. She really didn't want to leave Bridgeview just as her dreams here were coming true."

"I see. I'd love to have a look at it in that case, but it will have to wait until after the weekend. I need to finish packing and get moved before I have any free time after hours."

"I heard you're renting from Tad and Francesca. Nice suite."

Did everyone know everything about the other Bridgeview residents? That's what Adriana had said. Sounded like it wasn't an exaggeration. "Yes, they gave me a great deal and some incentive to move before the end of September."

"Sounds good. Once you get used to the dynamics of Bridgeview Elementary, I think you'll love it here. I don't blame Bianca Lopez for hating to leave. If I can spend my entire career in this one school, I'll retire happy."

Natasha Bertoli couldn't be a day over forty. Certainly no one had talked like that about his former school. Not that it had been a terrible place to work, at least until Dakota joined the staff. "Thanks. I appreciate the tip."

"No problem." Natasha turned away just as Myles's cell phone rang.

He tapped to accept the call and turned away from the window. "Myles Sheridan."

"Hi, Myles. This is Fran. I just wanted to let you know that I rounded up a few of my cousins to help you move on

Saturday. Some of the guys have trucks, and all of them have muscles. What time should they meet you in Spokane Valley?"

Myles blinked. All that because he'd mentioned he only had a small car and would need to rent a U-Haul truck for one day? "How many cousins do you have, anyway?"

She chuckled. "Quite a few, with a disproportionate number of them being guys in their twenties. Tad and our friend Wade Roper are in on it as well. Tad figures one trip will probably do it with that many of them."

"I don't know what to say." The vision of his weekend had just brightened considerably, though. He'd been certain he'd make the trek up and down the stairs a hundred times to load a moving truck, to say nothing of how he'd manage his few pieces of bulky furniture without help. He sure wasn't asking Dakota to give him a hand.

"Just say yes, and give me the time and the address. Better yet, text it to me so I can forward it to my cousins."

How much packing could he get done tonight and tomorrow? He'd need to finish the kitchen Saturday morning. "How about two o'clock? If you're sure it won't be an imposition."

"We're offering. Two o'clock sounds good."

"I'll pick up pizza or something for everyone afterward. It's the least I can do."

"Not a chance. You're moving to Bridgeview, Myles. Not that we don't eat pizza, but this is an opportunity for a group get together. A few of us will cover supper for the crew."

The Amato house wasn't that large, but the weather was still nice. Maybe Fran was planning to grill out. "Thank you. I can't tell you how much the support and help mean to me."

"Welcome to Bridgeview. And don't forget to text me the address in Spokane Valley."

Myles stared at his phone for a long moment after goodbyes had been said and the text sent. Just as Natasha had said, this was a real community. He was a stranger, and they welcomed him. Did they know he wasn't on board with their pet project yet? Would the welcome be revoked when they realized?

Chapter 4

*I*F YOU HAVE AN ULTERIOR MOTIVE, forget it."
Adriana narrowed her gaze at Fran. Her friends had taken
over her kitchen.

"I'm sorry. Asking you to host this seemed natural to me.
You've got the biggest house and that huge deck. Plus, you
always like to entertain."

All true. But Adriana couldn't help feeling out of control,
and it wasn't pleasant.

"Look, Rebekah told me Myles wasn't on board with the
whole garden thing at the school." Fran set her pot holders on
the counter and glanced at Rebekah. "I thought this would be
a good opportunity to show him how much food means to us
here. Real, garden-fresh, home cooked food. When he tastes
this meal—" she waved a hand to encompass the entire
kitchen "—he'll understand. I think of this impromptu get
together as a huge opportunity."

Adriana looked between her friends. Had she been
reading too much into it? After Rebekah's words the other
day, this had felt more like a set-up for romance than
education. "Oh. I guess that makes sense."

Funny how Rebekah was carefully not meeting her gaze, though. Instead, she bundled cutlery in cloth napkins at the island.

"So, I invited Nonna."

Adriana's gaze swung back to Fran. "You what?"

"We'll let her be the voice for the community. All someone needs to do is make a tiny mention about the curriculum, and Nonna will take it from there. No one else needs to say a thing, and he'll never know what hit him. Besides, she's bringing her sautéed green beans. Everyone loves those."

Fran's grandmother was a force to be reckoned with, for sure. Adriana could almost feel sorry for Myles. Mr. Sheridan. He *had* said he'd consider reworking his plan for the year, after all. Still, sic'ing Marietta on the poor man before he had a chance to blink seemed like cruel and unusual punishment. But... sautéed green beans? Yum.

A whimper came from the playpen in the dining room, and Violet popped through the archway. "Mom! Olivia's awake. Can I hold her?"

Rebekah washed and dried her hands. "I've got her for now, sweetie. She needs a diaper change and feeding."

"Then can I hold her?"

"For a few minutes. But it's not going to be right away. It takes her a long time to eat." Rebekah hurried into the other room. "Mama's here, baby girl. Come, let's get you a dry bottom." She scooped the infant and walked down the hallway to the bathroom, murmuring to the little one, with Violet dogging her heels.

Fran chuckled. "Motherhood has been good for Rebekah."

"It has." Adriana looked at the list on her whiteboard.

"Have you heard from Tad? What's left to do?"

"He texted a few minutes ago, just as they arrived back at the house to unload. I'd guess everyone will be here in an hour or so."

Adriana surveyed the kitchen. Fran had suggested they grill sliders, but with eight hungry men, Adriana convinced her they needed to be full-size burgers. The yeasty aroma of fresh-baked buns filled the air, vying with several plum pies that had followed the rolls out of the oven. If Daria and Marietta arrived soon with their contributions, everything would be covered. Even on short notice, they'd have a feast.

She turned to Fran. "Remember that night a few weeks ago when you guys came for dinner along with some of our other friends? The night Olivia was born?"

Fran nodded. "Homemade pasta. That was amazing. Now Tad thinks I should get one of those pasta roller gizmos. You've ruined him."

"Eden suggested I start charging for dinners here. Like, advertise and have complete strangers come in and help cook. She thinks people would be willing to pay for that kind of experience, and they'd learn about the local ingredients at the same time."

"That's an awesome idea. Are you going to? I mean, that blackberry goat cheese ice cream was divine. Your reputation would spread like wildfire."

"But this is more normal." Adriana waved her hand to encompass the kitchen. "It's just burgers and corn on the cob and a few salads."

"And lots of people haven't ever had homemade patties with whatever you mixed into the ground beef. To say nothing of the rolls you whipped up with only a few hours' warning."

"Why didn't you ask me yesterday? I'd have made sourdough instead."

Fran wiped her hands on a kitchen towel. "Because I thought you'd overthink it and cancel. Come up with some excuse, just like you tried a few minutes ago."

"Why would I?" It was true, though. Adriana didn't really want to get to know the man behind the teacher. He was too close to her age, too handsome, too good with the kids. He needed to stay distant so she could keep pushing him to make the changes.

But what if he did? Then she might suddenly find herself interested in romance again, which was a terrible idea for Violet's sake. The alternative was no garden component for her daughter's school year. No, surely there was another direction this could go.

Argh.

"I can see all the reasons chasing each other across your face, Adriana. You're an open book."

"Am not." At least, she'd better not be. She firmed her jaw.

The doorbell rang, and Marietta bustled in carrying a grocery bag with green beans sticking out the top. "There you are. Now you can help me trim the ends of the beans. You do have a large wok, don't you, Adriana? I will need it."

The Italian woman had to be over seventy-five and had been a widow for decades. Neither stopped her from interfering not just with her own extended family, but all of Bridgeview. Her vegetable garden still filled her backyard, and her pantry still bulged with gleaming quarts of tomatoes, sauces, and jellies. The woman had no idea how to take it easy, but she did know how to delegate. Or, at least, give orders.

"I can help trim for a few minutes, Marietta, but as soon as Tad calls Fran that the men are on their way over, I'll need to start the grill."

"Your girl can help."

"Violet?" Adriana's daughter was terrified of Marietta. "She's busy with something else right now. Here, let's see how much we can get done before the phone rings."

Fran gave Adriana a half grin and shook her head as she pulled several paring knives out of the drawer. Marietta dumped the bag of beans out onto the island, just missing the packages of cutlery.

Right. With Marietta, you got what she brought. And this time, they got to help with the beans. Adriana set her wok and largest frying pan on the stovetop, picked up a knife, and got to work.

"It's okay. There's no need to impose on anyone. I'll just get takeout tonight." Myles surveyed the piles of boxes stacked around the basement suite, his furniture roughly in the right places. It was going to be a while before this became his home.

"Fran won't take no for an answer."

That seemed to be a trait many Bridgeview women had in common. Or maybe it was women, in general. Running into Dakota in the parking lot at the apartment building had reminded him. She'd pressed him for his cell phone number so they could stay in touch. Uh, no. There'd been a good reason he'd never offered it to her before. Staying in touch was not an option.

He'd held out against Dakota, but there wasn't a good reason to annoy his landlady. If Fran wanted to feed him dinner tonight, he should welcome it after the busy day. Fran's cousins, all really nice guys he could envision being friends with, had already clomped up the stairs to the carport and rumbled off in their trucks.

"Come on." Tad jerked his chin to the carport where his vehicle waited. "I called to let Fran know we'd be there in a few minutes."

One last glance around the suite. His microwave was on the counter, but Myles had no clue where he'd find plates or forks... not that he'd need them for takeout. "Okay, thanks. I don't mean to be a bother."

Tad chuckled as he followed Myles up to the carport. "It was an invitation. Fran and her friends are a hospitable bunch. Plus, you deserve the food more than her cousins do."

Myles climbed into the passenger seat of Tad's truck. "Not sure about that. They pitched in to help a total stranger. They should get a reward."

"Not a stranger any longer." Tad backed out of the driveway. "I heard Peter asking you if you play basketball. Those guys eat, sleep, and breathe three-on-three."

"I've never been much into team sports." Give him a solo long distance swim or marathon bicycle ride anytime.

"I hear you. I wasn't much into sports before I married Fran. I'd still rather play soccer than basketball, though. Peter thought about kicking me out of the family on account of that."

Myles angled a glance at the other man.

"He was kidding. I think." Tad chuckled. The truck made a few more turns before pulling up in front of a sprawling contemporary house, larger than the usual war-era homes in the neighborhood.

"Where are we?" asked Myles.

"Sorry. This is Adriana's. Fran called her up to see if she could host. She has tons of space and loves to entertain."

"Adriana?" Myles should've stuck with takeout.

"Yes, Adriana Diaz. You must have met her by now? I think her daughter, Violet, is in your class."

"Oh, we've met." Had they ever. He couldn't very well insist on drive-through burgers now, though the temptation nearly overwhelmed him along with exhaustion.

"Good. We've known her for years, since before her husband died. Stephan was one of the good ones. It's been a rough time for her, single parent and all."

"I'm sure." Myles followed Tad up the walk between giant rhododendron bushes then into the house. It seemed even bigger inside than out with light flowing in from the tall windows in the dining room beside the foyer. Draperies framed the view of a spacious backyard with an open-weave fence between it and the river.

Adriana also stood framed in those windows. She laughed at Fran's cousin Basil from beside the grill as he snapped a pair of tongs in her direction. The scent of burgers wafted in through the open patio door.

He was starving.

"Hi, Tad." Fran kissed her husband then smiled at Myles. "Welcome to Adriana's house. She's out back. Food's nearly ready."

Wade Roper, who'd spent the afternoon hauling cardboard boxes in his pickup, cradled a tiny baby against his chest in some kind of carrier. Four boys, one of them Sam, stampeded past and out into the yard. Women's voices came from the kitchen to his left, along with a few enticing smells

Myles couldn't place.

"Come on out back." Tad motioned toward the patio doors.

Did he have to? This felt like crashing someone else's family reunion. Apparently that's what he'd done by accepting a job at Bridgeview Elementary, though. And then renting the Amatos' suite. This was merely a result of the earlier two decisions.

Myles followed Tad past a polished walnut dining room table with a cream-colored cloth running down it. A bouquet of colorful flowers in an old rusty pitcher sat in the middle. The combination was as unexpected as the woman who lived here.

Adriana glanced over, her face slightly flushed. Likely from standing over the grill. "Welcome to our house, Mr. Sheridan." She smiled, but it didn't quite reach her eyes.

"Thanks for the invitation, Ms. Diaz." It likely hadn't been her idea.

"What's with the formality?" Tad laughed as he looked between them. "This isn't school, and you both have first names."

Myles didn't dare meet Adriana's gaze. "That's the context where we met." He needed to keep that in mind, not notice how much more engaging she seemed here on her own turf. Her long hair streamed down the back of her short-sleeved blue top. Not that he noticed the fit of her jeans on her long legs.

"I can do it if he can," she said, chuckling. "Are you up for it? Myles?"

He jerked his gaze back to her face. "Adriana. I think I can remember that." There was no chance of him forgetting. Not when she let loose and laughed like that.

45

Chapter 5

ARIETTA BUSTLED OUT ONTO the deck carrying a large bowl of sautéed green beans. She set it in the middle of the patio table after moving a few other dishes out of the way. "There. We're ready now."

Adriana bit back a grin. Everything else had been on the table five minutes ago, and the kids swarmed the area like starving puppies. "Tad, would you say grace?"

She didn't miss seeing Myles's head jerk up as he looked straight at her. Well, too bad. This was her home, and she and her friends were Christians. If he didn't want his food blessed, that was his problem. It would make it easier for her to keep the barrier up between them.

Wait. Seriously? That's how she wanted him to see her? Not as a gentle, loving believer, but as an antagonistic mother? Because that would go a long way to drawing him to faith in Jesus. Being Christlike wasn't for the benefit of a possible relationship — where was that thought even coming from? — but for the man's eternal destiny.

"...in Jesus' name, amen."

Adriana scrunched her eyes shut for another second then opened them again, heat flooding her face. She'd spent the entire prayer staring at Myles, just as he'd spent it staring at her. He still was.

She gave her head a quick shake. "Okay, everyone. Grab a plate and help yourself. Sit anywhere you like — at the table inside, over on the deck chairs, or down in the yard."

Sam and Caden, Marco and Daria's oldest, were big enough to dish themselves up. Somehow they were first in line, Violet elbowing them for room.

Adriana put her hand on her daughter's shoulder. "May I help you?"

Violet frowned as she examined the table laden with various salads the other women had brought. "I just want a burger. No relish or mustard."

"Choose one other food, too, please. Those green beans are delicious. Or a scoop of salad?"

Violet wrinkled her nose. "Corn. I guess."

"Okay." Adriana was in no mood to fight with her daughter. She loaded the plate and passed it to Violet, who carried it down to the yard and joined the boys.

When everyone had dished up, the chatter on the deck settled into a hum that rolled over Adriana like a pleasant ripple. She checked the status of all the serving dishes.

"Where do you go to church?"

Adriana, her back to the group, froze at Myles's voice.

"Bridgeview Bible," Tad responded. Whew, the question hadn't been aimed at her. "It's a community church over on West Main."

"Must be a pretty big church."

47

Tad chuckled. "To house this crew and then some? It's a nice size. Big enough to be healthy, small enough to know nearly everyone."

"I'll give it a try tomorrow. I've been a bit concerned about leaving my church in Spokane Valley behind."

Adriana turned to see the two men, plates balanced on their knees as they sat on the steps overlooking the yard. Little Luca sat pressed between them.

"Always room for one more." Tad chomped into his corn on the cob.

"Come. Bring food and sit down," Marietta ordered. "Always with the hovering."

"Be right there." They should have done sliders, after all. The burgers were too big for the tightness in Adriana's gut, to say nothing of all the delicious side dishes. She grabbed a patty with no bun and added a small scoop of green beans, Fran's pasta salad, and Rebekah's green salad to her plate before taking a spot on the deck far from the boisterous cousins. Somehow that put her with the back steps in full view. Purely by accident.

"So that's the new teacher?" Marietta jabbed her fork toward Myles.

"Yes, it is." Fran tossed an amused grin at Adriana. "Didn't Tad introduce you?"

"No. They must have come in while I was cooking. What was the school board thinking, hiring a man to teach small children?"

"Why not?" Daria leaned closer. "Caden is sorry he missed the experience."

"Sam, too," admitted Adriana. Both boys were in third grade with Natasha Bertoli.

"What can a man know about children that young?"

Did Myles's back stiffen, or was that Adriana's imagination?

"It's the twenty-first century, Nonna." Fran patted her grandmother's arm. "Dads are far more involved with their little kids than they were in your day. Look. Wade's got Olivia in the baby carrier. Marco's down in the yard with Caden and Oren. And Tad is helping Luca with his food, leaving the mothers to eat in peace. They know we all worked hard to put dinner on the table. Besides, they genuinely like spending time with their kids."

"But *he* doesn't have children." Marietta thrust her chin toward Myles's back. "Does he?"

Myles rose and turned, facing the women. His eyes ranged across the group, pausing for a few seconds on Adriana before settling on the older woman. "I'm Myles Sheridan, second grade teacher. And you are...?"

"Marietta Santoro." She gestured around the backyard. "Most of these are my grandchildren. My great-grandchildren."

He reached down and shook her hand. "I'm so pleased to meet you."

After what he'd overheard? Yeah, sure. Somehow he'd managed to place a sincere-looking smile on his face.

Marietta harrumphed and shook her finger at him. "It's not natural, a man with the little ones. We'll be watching."

"Oh, Nonna. He'll be fine." Fran's fingers soothed her grandmother's arm. "I think it's positive for the children to have a good male role model. Don't you agree, Adriana?"

Adriana gulped. All eyes swung to her, including Myles's. "Definitely." What else was she supposed to say? Fran would get an earful later for putting her on the spot like this.

Fran turned to Myles. "Filling Bianca Lopez's shoes must seem daunting at times. She'd been in that classroom for fifteen years and was well-loved by everyone."

A few seconds ago he'd looked amused at Adriana's discomfort. Now his eyes grew wary. "I've heard nothing but good about her."

"She was the teacher liaison for the greenhouse project. Absolutely one of her passions. I imagine she left lesson ideas for you."

Adriana stared at her plate, from which she'd taken only a few bites. All appetite fled. Cornering Myles at the school had been one thing, but listening to Fran's maneuvering now made her gut clench. The topic was as crucial as it had ever been, but this wasn't the time or the place.

"I'm not sure yet, to be honest. My plans didn't include that sort of focus—"

"What is this? The community has worked hard to get that greenhouse for the school." Marietta glared at Myles. "We expect to have it used."

Myles tipped his head toward the old woman. "So I've come to understand."

Adriana just bet he had.

"Ms. Bertoli offered me Mrs. Lopez's research. Several boxes full and overflowing." Myles's hands measured out several cubic feet of space. "I haven't had time to dig into them yet with moving and all."

Marietta snorted. "You need to get on it before the weather changes."

Myles glanced at Adriana for an instant. "I'll keep that in mind." He strode over to the table and helped himself to another small scoop of beans. "These are great. Compliments to the cook."

Adriana bit back a grin. How far would that go to placating Marietta? And why did it even matter?

If Adriana hadn't set Fran up to trigger that rude old woman, she'd been in on it. Why else wouldn't she meet his gaze? Her house, her guests, her rules. And what a house. Any little dreams that had begun to bubble up about this woman needed to sink right back down into the muck from which they'd come.

Myles wasn't in this league, not on his teacher's salary. His mom had kept the modest family home after his parents' split when he was a teen, but he'd felt more comfortable in his dad's apartment than where Mom had spewed venom at every mention of his father. An apartment, a basement suite — those were good enough for him. A nice house didn't bring happiness.

And marriages didn't last. Look at his parents. Look at his older brother, Keith. Even look at Adriana, widowed so young.

No, he shouldn't be looking at Adriana, even as she brought out a tray with several fragrant pies. Another woman — Marco's wife, Daria? It was hard to keep them all straight — followed with a bucket and a stack of plates.

"Would you like plum pie and homemade ice cream?" Adriana's voice came from right by his shoulder.

"I, uh... thank you. Sounds good."

"Sorry about Marietta," she said quietly. "She does have a heart of gold, but she doesn't reveal it easily."

A heart of gold? Myles raised his eyebrows. Yeah, right.

"I can see it's hard to believe, but it's still true."

"I'll reserve judgment."

She leaned a little closer. "No matter what it might seem like, I didn't put her up to that. Promise."

Myles's eyes caught on hers and sank in their depths. He shouldn't believe her, but somehow he did. She was a concerned mom, not an enemy. Not just a mother. A woman.

Basil slung his arm across Adriana's shoulders. "That pie smells awesome. Did you make it?"

"I did." Adriana shifted slightly, and Basil's arm fell. "I'll dish up a few pieces if you'd like to scoop ice cream."

"Uh, sure." Basil offered Myles a sardonic grin. "Always glad to help a pretty woman."

Basil was just a kid compared to Adriana. A cocky, smooth-talking youth who didn't seem to notice he'd been brushed off. But how old was Adriana? Maybe Myles was just a kid in her eyes, too, but somehow he didn't think so. Not with the way she looked at him. With awareness.

He was her daughter's teacher. There weren't any rules governing whom he dated, but anyone could see it would be awkward to get involved with the mother of one of his students, especially a child as volatile as Violet. No, pursuing Adriana was a bad idea on so many levels. Besides, he was fine staying single.

Myles could keep telling himself that, but even he wasn't buying it.

Basil delivered pieces of pie to the women first, and the fruity aroma rich with cinnamon and cloves wafted past Myles. "Smells really good."

She flashed him a smile. "Here, take the next one."

"I can wait my turn."

"And I say it's your turn now." Adriana held a plate toward him.

"Thanks." He stood watching her as the ice cream melted into tiny rivulets flowing down the rich purple fruit. "Also thanks for hosting this dinner. I was going to order pizza for the guys for helping."

"Fran asked me to, but I was happy to agree. I've felt for a long time that God gave me this home for a reason, and that's to share it with others. Also, I love to have people over. Love cooking."

Myles looked over the remains of the meal. "Everything tasted awesome. Better than takeout, for sure."

"The others pitched in with the side dishes. Consider it a 'Welcome to Bridgeview' dinner."

"Are *you*... welcoming me?" Myles held his breath. Why had he said that? He knew better. He did.

Her chin came up slightly as she reached for the next pie, not meeting his gaze. "I'm welcoming you to the community as my daughter's teacher." She slid a few more plates toward the end of the table where Basil gathered them up.

Conversation and laughter swirled around them, but Myles felt rooted to the spot, watching her.

"Mom, can I have some pie?" Violet's head rammed into Myles's elbow.

"Did you finish your food?"

"Duke ate it."

Adriana gave her daughter her full attention for a few seconds. "Did you leave your plate on the ground while you played?"

A dog the size of a pony could help himself right off the dinner table without stretching. What was he, a Great Pyrenees or something?

53

Violet shrugged. "Can I have pie now?"

"No, you may not. You know the rules."

"But I want a piece. Sam got one."

"Your brother ate all his dinner. He even had seconds. No more arguing, Violet. If you're hungry, go pull some carrots from the garden."

The little girl scowled and stomped away.

Myles took a second look at the backyard. A few chickens pecked in a raised bed that was covered in netting. Other fowl strutted around an enclosed pen off to the side. More garden beds overflowed with fresh produce, and several fruit trees lined the other edge of the property right down to the riverfront fence, two of them laden with small purple orbs.

Her demands didn't come from a vacuum. She lived what she asked him to teach.

He pointed at the plum tree, a suspicion growing. "Did your pie ingredients grow here?" Somehow he'd assumed the desserts were from the supermarket or maybe the neighborhood bakery. He'd driven past Bridgeview Bakery and Bistro but hadn't had a chance to stop in yet.

"Yes, the plums are from my trees."

Myles scanned the table. "The beans?"

"Marietta's garden. Rebekah picked up the ingredients for her salad at the farmers market. Fran's and Daria's are a mix of homegrown and store-bought." Her eyes measured him. "I think I told you we believe in real food in this neighborhood."

He nodded slowly. "I'm beginning to see what you mean."

Chapter 6

ADRIANA NUDGED OPEN THE DOOR to the school greenhouse and peered inside. Surely she wasn't the only parent to respond to Myles's request for help sorting out his classroom's sections of the garden and greenhouse.

Her gut soured. No, there was another. Catalina Romero stood a little too close to Myles, who seemed backed into a corner. Myles's gaze snapped over to the door and he gave Adriana a small smile. "Adri... Ms. Diaz. I'm so glad you could make it."

Catalina turned, and her gaze narrowed. "Adriana."

"Hi, Catalina. Here to help Mr. Sheridan get set up?" Or, maybe, for some other reason. Why else would the woman be dressed in a too-tight tank that revealed her midriff?

"Yes. And you?"

"The same." Adriana offered a bright smile. "I didn't realize you were into gardening. That's terrific."

"Just because the kids and I live in an apartment doesn't mean we don't enjoy the finer things in life." Catalina cast an appraising eye over Myles as she chewed a wad of gum.

The man had the grace to flush as he edged past her. Not that she gave him space to do so without brushing against her. "So, let's get started. Our classroom has been assigned the space next to the door. I have to admit that Mrs. Lopez left so many notes it's difficult to diffuse them into a plan of action. She was quite enthusiastic."

"She was our most avid supporter within the school." Adriana dared a peek at Myles. How many ways could her priorities be pulled? But that was silly. She only had one, and that was to make sure her kids grew up into well-rounded adults who loved Jesus.

"We know you'll do a great job, though." Catalina shifted between them.

Adriana shook her head. Catalina dating Myles was an even worse idea. That woman had been on the manhunt since her husband left several years before.

Myles cast a pleading look over Catalina's shoulder at Adriana. "Ms. Bertoli said her class had planted a fall garden a month ago. Out in the garden beds. Maybe we could have a look."

He was going to have to learn to deal with mothers like Catalina. A sudden thought struck Adriana. *She* wasn't that bad, was she? No, of course not. She wasn't actually interested in Myles herself. She hadn't given another man a second thought since she and Stephan had begun dating in college. Not before his death, and not after.

Adriana led the way back out of the greenhouse. This little attraction was just a sign she was still alive. It didn't mean she and Myles... She felt him beside her and glanced up into his intense blue eyes. Oh, man. If he'd looked at Catalina the same way, no wonder the other mom was falling all over him. Which only proved how awkward this all was.

A parent dating her child's teacher only set everyone up for problems.

She pointed over at the raised bed where Sam's class had been working. Carrots, radishes, and kale — barely two inches tall — poked out amid weeds. Her fingers itched to pull the weeds and thin the crowded plants.

"Is it too late for anything to grow? If we planted next week?" Myles spoke from so close to her shoulder that she jumped.

Too late for anything to grow? Why did that seem laden with double meanings? No, she was totally reading things into an innocent conversation about seeds.

"My kids don't really like vegetables." Catalina popped her bubblegum.

"That's one of the reasons the PTA worked so hard for the school garden. Children are much more likely to eat foods they've helped to grow. This project will give them lifelong skills and set them up for healthier habits."

"Mrs. Lopez's notes had some recipes in them." Myles looked thoughtful. "I could send some of those home with the students."

"You could." There might even be some new ones in the bunch.

"So, what do you want us to do?" Catalina rested her hand on Myles's arm.

Someone was going to have to take charge here, and it obviously wasn't going to be Myles. Adriana pointed at the bed labeled '2.' "You can bring the children out here and ask them to pull the weeds that have grown up in that bed over the summer. Maybe get a weed chart and get them to see how many types there are and which are edible. Stuff like that. Then when it's been cleared, you can do a soil test. I'm pretty sure there are some kits in the cupboard in the greenhouse. Teach them a bit about pH."

"An introduction to chemistry." Myles nodded thoughtfully.

There was chemistry, and then there was chemistry. She blinked and continued. "It's not too late to plant a few cool weather crops like Ms. Bertoli's students have done. In fact, it might be interesting to both classes to see the differences between the plants sown earlier and those sown later. How does the weather affect their growth? That kind of thing."

"Sky isn't going to like coming home covered in dirt," said Catalina.

He'd probably like it just fine. His older siblings might not, but that problem lay with their teachers, not Myles. "A little dirt does a child good. It builds antibodies, strengthening their immune system."

"So I've heard," Myles put in.

Catalina's gum snapped, breaking the moment once again. "So what are we doing here today? Aren't we spending some time together, working on stuff?" She waggled her eyebrows at Myles.

He looked back and forth between them, settling on Adriana. "I thought we'd get things cleaned up and ready, but you think the students should do that."

She shrugged. "It will give them ownership. Plus, there are so many little lessons that can be tucked in here and there. They'll benefit from doing the work."

"I understand Bridgeview Elementary welcomes parents in the classroom. You wouldn't, by any chance, be free on Tuesday afternoons? That's the time assigned to our class out here."

Adriana had a stack of invoices to enter for the bakery, to say nothing of draperies to complete and install for the Ridleys over on West Riverside. A couple of hours out wouldn't set either project behind enough to matter, though. Not when she was dedicated to making Violet's school year as solid as possible. It had nothing at all to do with spending time with Myles Sheridan.

Nothing at all.

Myles stood in front of his class on Tuesday afternoon with Adriana and Catalina on either side of him. Of course Sky's mother had volunteered when Adriana agreed.

He'd spent the entire weekend digging through all the material Bianca Lopez had left him. Three large boxes had been filled with everything from random internet printouts to packages of seeds and garden gloves much too small for him and too large for his young students. He'd sorted the papers into seasonal piles, though he wasn't certain of his accuracy.

Any lesson plan she'd created was either fully in her head or with her in Boston.

He took a deep breath. "Okay, this afternoon we're going to be working in the garden. I hope you all remembered to wear play clothes." He divided the students into three teams and assigned an adult to each, trying to ignore the panicky feeling of being out of control. Why, again, was he sliding down the slippery slope to giving in? He didn't want to garden. He wanted to run his own classroom, not be pushed into a lesson plan he was making up on the fly and had no idea how to implement.

59

All his life he'd done his best to live up to expectations. He'd studied hard to make his parents proud and avoided conflict wherever possible. That was why.

Adriana led her chattering group out the door, a more sullen Catalina behind her. Myles forced a smile to the remaining students. "All right. Let's go."

Violet glared at him, arms crossed. "I want to be with my mom."

"You're with me." Better she grouched at him than at Sky's mother. Catalina had seemed to pick up on vibes between him and Adriana the other day, and he couldn't trust her not to take it out on Violet. He'd put Sky with Adriana, though.

"I don't want to."

"If you'd prefer to spend garden time in the counselor's office, I can arrange that. The rest of us will be outside."

The child narrowed her eyes at him, chin set. Finally she turned and flounced her way out the door.

Myles gestured for the rest of his group to follow her. This wasn't the first time Violet had challenged him in the class. The girl had issues. *Lord, how am I going to deal with her? And what am I going to do with my attraction to her mother?*

The answer to the second question was simple. Nothing. He couldn't imagine the awkwardness of a relationship with the mother of one of his students, no matter how intriguing he found her. The answer to the first question was the one that ought to occupy his mind.

Out in the garden, Adriana held up a tall weed with scalloped spearhead-shaped leaves. "This one is called lamb's quarters. Can anyone guess why?" She passed it to Sky, who turned it over and handed it to the next child.

The children shook their heads.

"I don't know, either." Adriana chuckled. "But look around at the gardens and see how many of these you can spot. Although we usually consider them to be weeds, they're actually edible. Anyone want to try a bite?" She tore off a leaf and popped it in her mouth.

Myles blinked. The children stared.

Adriana's mouth pursed. "Somewhat bitter. The smaller leaves are generally milder in flavor. So, today we are going to pull every single plant out of this garden." She indicated the long bed made of corrugated metal held in place with four-by-four posts. "But we are not just going to throw them away. We're going to put them in piles with others like them, and talk about each. I don't want you to assume that just because it grows in the garden it's edible. Some plants will make your tummies sick, so always make sure. Okay?" She lay the lamb's quarters on a rock off to the side. "Everyone find a place around the bed and put your gloves on. Then reach in at the base of a plant and pull it carefully, trying not to break it off. Like this." She demonstrated. "Then let's see what we find."

Myles became aware of Catalina at his elbow. "Who put her in charge? You'd think she was the teacher or something."

He shifted slightly away. "I asked her to. She knows far more about this than I do. Why don't you take your group around the other side of the bed?"

She looked at him with narrowed eyes before doing as he asked.

Myles arranged the remaining children around the south end of the garden bed, as far as he could get from either woman. "Have any of you ever eaten lamb's quarters?"

Violet rolled her eyes at him. "Of course I have.

Sometimes Mom cooks them like spinach."

He couldn't help himself. "Do you like spinach?"

"No, it's totally yuck. But I don't get dessert if I don't have a few bites."

It was good to know someone could make Violet do something she didn't want to. He was nearly at his wit's end some days in the classroom. He turned to the other children. "Anyone else try it before?"

When all the heads around him shook, he reached for a leaf growing in front of him, plucked it, and put it in his mouth. Gross. It was all he could do not to spit it back out. That was the most disgusting thing he'd ever tasted. He'd take Adriana's word for it that the flavor was milder if the plant were younger. No way was he going near the stuff again, other than to pull it and toss it in the compost.

He'd learned that much from Bianca's notes. Compost, not garbage can. The learning curve was just beginning.

From the other end of the long bed, he listened to Adriana explain the properties of another plant to the wide-eyed children.

Much as he wanted to get involved — for the first time in his life — he'd chosen the wrong woman to become interested in. No way could he act on his fascination.

She met his gaze down the long garden bed.

There had to be some way to get through this school year without tumbling into the pitfalls lining the path.

Chapter 7

*T*HIS IS CRAZY." Adriana paced her living room. It was a rainy, windy day in early October, and she already missed hanging out with Rebekah and baby Olivia on the wide back deck.

Rebekah held Olivia against her shoulder, patting the baby's back. "I wish I could advise you to go for it."

Adriana pivoted, hands on her hips. "You did advise that. Weeks ago."

"I know, but it was all hilariously hypothetical then. I didn't think you and Myles would actually—"

"I know." The thought was still rather shocking to Adriana, too. "Trust me. It can't be any weirder to you than it is to me. I thought Stephan was it for me, and I was okay with that. Sure, I've been lonely at times, but only for him, you know? Not for a new relationship with another man. It feels somehow disloyal."

Olivia gurgled out a belch, and Rebekah caught the spit with a cloth before snuggling the infant back to her breast. "It's been five years."

In just a matter of weeks, it would be. It seemed like

63

yesterday. It seemed like another lifetime. It seemed like something that had happened in a movie to someone else.

Adriana stared at the collage of family portraits on the wall. Her and Stephan's wedding day. Another of Sam, barely able to sit up by himself. A family photo where Sam, a year and a half old, sat on her lap while Stephan cradled the newborn Violet, unable to take his eyes off his daughter. More photos from a shoot two years later, the summer before Stephan died. The kids' school pictures.

She needed to book a photographer again. Her mom had been after her for a new family photo for their wall. She and the kids were a family now. Without Stephan. Without anyone new added.

Myles.

Her friend was right. Myles, with his brown hair and beard, his twinkling blue eyes, his soft smile, was a bad idea.

"If he wasn't Violet's teacher, I wouldn't have any concerns," Rebekah said quietly over the baby's sucking sounds. "And long term, I don't. The school doesn't have a specific policy forbidding teachers from dating each other or the parent of one of their students, but it's frowned on."

Rebekah would know about the ins and outs of teacher protocol. She'd been a counselor at Bridgeview Elementary before Olivia's birth.

"I only volunteered to help with the garden to keep him on track. I didn't mean for this to happen."

"We never do." Her friend chuckled. "Love kind of sneaks up on us."

Adriana narrowed her gaze. "I didn't say anything about love."

"I know it's early yet. You only met him a month ago."

"Six weeks." Why had she even bothered to make the

correction? It must sound like she'd been counting the days. "That's how long it's been since the school year started."

"Tell yourself what you need to hear. Myles seems like a great guy. Juanita was telling me how much Sabrina likes him. Heather Sund told me Desiree has a serious crush on him. What does Violet think?"

"She doesn't say much. They're painting vegetable portraits for the new community center's grand opening in a couple of weeks. She's pretty stoked about that."

"Vegetable portraits?" Rebekah's eyebrows rose. "What is Violet painting?"

"An eggplant, she says."

"An *eggplant*? I bet half those kids have never even met one."

"Probably true. But they grew well in our garden this summer, and the kids decided they liked them grilled with olive oil and herbs and smeared on crackers." Adriana laughed. "Before that, we were all about carrots and cucumbers around here. I'm thankful she and Sam gave eggplant a try. It opened up additional possibilities."

Rebekah disengaged the baby and began patting her back again.

"Oh, let me." Adriana draped the flannel cloth over her shoulder and picked up Olivia. "Here you go, baby girl. Get the rumblies out of your tummy."

"Holding a baby looks good on you. Were you and Stephan planning on another?"

"We'd barely gotten any sleep in the two years since Violet's birth. Sam was such an easy baby in comparison. So it was in discussion."

"You're not too old to have more."

The words hung in the living room, punctuated only by

rain on the metal roof of the deck just beyond the windows.

"I'm thirty-four, Rebekah. It may not be too old, but it feels like it." Myles was so good with the students. He'd be a great dad. He deserved to be one. "That's another good reason I shouldn't date Myles."

Rebekah shook her head. "I think I missed something in translation."

"I don't know how old he is, but for men it doesn't matter so much. He should marry a woman young enough to give him babies. What guy wants to be a stepdad instead of a biological father?"

"And yet, from what you've said, it's you he's got eyes for."

Adriana shook her head. "It can't work."

"Not everything in life can be measured by logic." Rebekah rose and adjusted her clothing. "I'm getting a glass of water. Want one?"

"There's iced tea in the fridge if you'd rather."

"Okay, I'll bring you one, too."

Adriana nuzzled Olivia's soft cheek and inhaled the sweet smell of baby. The downy hair on the infant's head reminded her of Sam's. Violet's had been darker. Fuller. "What do you think, baby girl?" she murmured. "I've never been much of one for just going with the flow. I like logic. Numbers. Validated results. That's why I'm a bookkeeper. As a seamstress, I can exercise more creativity, but there are still rules if I want the item to work as a duvet cover, as draperies, as a skirt."

Ice clinked into glasses in the kitchen. The fridge door opened and closed.

She swayed, snuggling the baby. "Tell me what to do, Olivia."

The infant squirmed, pushed her fist into her mouth, and began sucking noisily as she drooped back to sleep.

"You're a lucky baby. You have a mommy and a daddy who love you and take care of you. Someday, you'll have to make tough decisions, too, but not for a long time." Oh, it wasn't luck. It was God's design. Rebekah and Wade had gone through some really rough patches — even breaking up for four years — before finding their way to a happy marriage.

The outside door slammed and Violet and Sam clattered into the kitchen.

"They should just shut up!" Violet stormed.

Uh oh.

"You have to tell them not to talk like that anymore," Sam insisted.

"What's up, guys?" Rebekah asked. "Want a glass of iced tea?"

Adriana should go into the kitchen and dig out the after-school snack she'd prepared. But would Violet tell Rebekah what the problem was? The little girl had been increasingly grumpy over the past couple of weeks, and that was saying something. She wasn't a particularly sunny child to begin with.

"You don't even know," Violet said.

Her hands probably rested on her hips as she glared at her brother, but Adriana stayed standing behind the dividing wall.

"It works. Right, Mrs. Roper? That's what we got taught in bully-proof. Nobody picks on me anymore."

Good to know.

"Sure it works. The other kids will only bug you if you make it fun for them, Violet. If you tell them the game is over, they'll learn to respect that."

"Easy for you to say. You're not in Mr. Sheridan's class. They're not making fun of *you* because they think he likes Mom!"

Adriana froze, her hand barely touching Olivia's back. Oh, man. Should she go in the kitchen and tell Violet it wasn't true, and not to worry about it? And yet... she suspected the opposite. That Myles *did* like her. That she liked him back. How could the other students have picked up on that? She'd tried so hard to hide it, even from herself.

On Tuesday afternoon, Adriana was all business. Myles tried to put his finger on what was different. It wasn't that she'd cast him moony eyes before, but now she kept her distance, almost like he didn't exist.

He existed. This was his classroom. His students. His garden bed.

There wasn't much to do in the garden right now. Carrots, radishes, and spinach peeked through the soil, but it was anyone's guess if the heavy frosts — or even snow — would kill the tiny plants before they had a chance to flourish. Adriana said the sheltered location of the garden would help, as would the crop cover, which seemed thinner than a bed sheet.

Adriana said. He had to bite off those words constantly when talking to anyone else. Her name kept bubbling into his mouth.

He strolled over to the garden shed just as the class headed back inside. "Adriana? Can we talk? Maybe later, after school."

She set the last trowel onto its hook and glanced at him. "Is it my kid? What's she done now?"

"No. It's not Violet."

"Then…" Her voice trailed away as she focused on his face.

For one brief moment, he lost himself in her brown eyes. How had he never noticed that fleck of gold before? Her straight nose, high cheekbones, unblemished skin. A few tendrils of hair had pulled loose from her long ponytail and curled around her face. Her lips tightened as he took them in, and his guilty gaze swung back to her eyes.

"I-I wanted to talk about the next few weeks of garden time." No, he didn't. He wanted to tell her he thought she was amazing. A superb help with the class, a great mom to a difficult child, but more than that. That he found her attractive. That he wanted to get to know her, spend time with her, find out if she felt the same way. See if anything more might grow.

"Garden time?" She repeated.

Myles blinked. "Uh, yes. I had some ideas. There's a pumpkin farm just north of the city. I was thinking about a field trip. Would that be appropriate?"

"Sure. Sounds good."

He became aware of birds chirping. The only sound. He turned and looked around as the last child disappeared into the school. Catalina held the door, her gaze narrowed as she watched them.

Uh oh. He knew better than to pull anything personal into school time. But he hadn't, not really. All they'd talked about was the class garden. A gentleman regardless, he gestured for Adriana to precede him toward the building.

"I don't think I can make it back at two-forty-five," she

said quietly. "But go ahead and put your thoughts into an email. I know you have all the parents' contact information on file."

He nodded as she brushed past him on the narrow path between the beds. "I can do that." He caught the door Catalina still braced open. "I've got it." He smiled down at Sky's mom.

Catalina's eyebrows rose and her mouth tightened. Seeing her lips did not evoke the same sensation as noticing Adriana's. Not that he'd needed any further confirmation that he was falling for Violet's mother.

Catalina followed Adriana and the students down the corridor and into the classroom, where Sky and a few others had gathered around a flushed-looking Violet. The group scattered as the adults entered, but Violet stared straight ahead, not looking at her mom or at him.

What was going on? Had he missed something? Violet wasn't the most socially adapted child in the room. Her prickly nature constantly built a hedge between her and the others — sometimes even between her and her best friends, Sabrina and Desiree. He'd keep a closer watch, and see what he could do to help her.

"Say thanks to Ms. Romero and Ms. Diaz for helping us in the garden today, and then we'll get out our art projects."

The children chorused their gratitude.

Myles didn't let his gaze linger as Adriana followed Catalina out of the classroom. She'd offered he could send an email, and he'd take her up on it. He'd find a way to get to know her. Find out if there really was a spark, and not some awkward thing only he imagined.

Chapter 8

*T*HE CHILDREN WERE IN BED, the chickens tucked in their coop, and Duke lay sprawled on the floor by her feet. Adriana stared at her laptop and read Myles's email one more time.

It started promising with, "Dear Adriana," but from there it stayed well within the bounds of teacher-parent. What had she expected? That he'd been about to ask her out or something? That he'd pour out his feelings like some kind of love-starved teenager writing desperately emotive poetry?

"Duke? Have I been reading something into this? Something that isn't real?" That would be just her luck. Finally ready to move forward and believe that love might find her for a second time… and be stupid enough to turn her affection on someone who was only being polite.

The gentle giant at her feet opened his eyes but didn't twitch.

But then, what of the children teasing Violet? Adriana hadn't confronted her daughter or let her know what she'd overheard a few days back. Sam hadn't blabbed, either. If the kids in the classroom had caught the undercurrents, Adriana had to believe they were real.

She set the laptop aside and headed into the kitchen for a fresh cup of tea and two of the pumpkin oatmeal cookies she'd made yesterday. Fortified, she curled back up in the easy chair, tucked the quilt over her, and had a nibble of cookie before pulling the laptop closer and rereading his words.

Myles thanked her for her faithful help. Let her know that there would be a school-wide scarecrow-making contest soon. She'd had an official letter from Natasha, Sam's teacher, already. It was good the second graders would participate.

He sent her the link for the pumpkin farm and wondered if making jack-o'-lanterns was an appropriate use of garden class time for the last Tuesday of October.

And he signed the email, "Yours, Myles."

He wasn't hers. He'd left little room in the few short paragraphs for any romantic interpretation.

Rebekah's gentle warning nudged her brain. Myles wouldn't do anything inappropriate. Nothing to feed the antagonism of Catalina Romero and others like her. Even the children teasing Violet, if he knew about that.

"Duke? Seriously, I could use some help here. Why did I choose this man to let behind my defenses? Why somebody so complicated? Why not a... an electrician, or a used car salesman, or somebody else completely ordinary? Why my child's teacher?"

The dog rose and nudged the laptop aside with his huge head.

Adriana took the hint and set it on the side table before wrapping her arms around Duke's neck. The soft fur warmed her cheek and soothed her, his doggy scent that of fallen autumn leaves and an unauthorized swim in the river. One of the kids must have left the gate open.

He licked her ear, and she pulled away, cradling his great head between her hands. "Oh, Duke." She kissed his nose and was rewarded with another quick flick of his tongue.

When the dog wandered over to the doors to the deck and looked over his shoulder at her, she grabbed a warm jacket and followed him outside. She stared at the mist rising from the river not far beyond while he did his business down beside the back fence.

She and Stephan had often sat on this deck, encased in fog so dense they could hardly see each other. They'd snuggled and talked about the past, the future, their dreams. All she had now were memories.

Do not remember the former things, nor consider the things of old. Behold, I will do a new thing.

Where was that in the Bible? She should know, though it likely had nothing to do with remembering a former marriage. A good marriage with a good man. It would be wrong to forget Stephan. For the kids' sake. For her own sake. He was part of her. Always would be, but she didn't have to dwell in the past. She could accept a new thing from God, couldn't she?

But how would she know if Myles was her future? Even the thought seemed silly. They barely knew each other. He'd never said a word to give this idea anything to hinge on. It was only the way his eyes lingered on her, his smile just that little bit more.

Guessing games like back in junior high. *Does he like me? He said "hi" in the hallway. He must like me.*

Adriana groaned and huddled in her coat. She didn't want to feel fourteen again. Didn't want to relive the early college days with Stephan, though he hadn't made her wonder for long. Stephan had been strong. Decisive. He'd swept her off her feet. Five years after his death, her feet were firmly planted back on terra firma. Her memories had been enough.

Until Myles.

Duke bounded out of the mist and up the steps. Adriana held the door for him and followed him back inside. She picked up the laptop and opened a new browser tab to search for the verse that had come to mind. There it was, in her favorite translation, The Voice. Isaiah 43:18-19.

Don't revel only in the past, or spend all your time recounting the victories of days gone by. Watch closely: I am preparing something new; it's happening now, even as I speak, and you're about to see it. I am preparing a way through the desert; waters will flow where there had been none.

The margin notes reminded her this was The Eternal One speaking to the children of Israel about their ancestors' great exodus from Egypt. They didn't need to live in the past to remember God's glory. He had something in store for them, right then. In present time.

"Do you have something planned for me, Lord? Help me to respect the past but move into the future You have created for me. Whether it's with Myles or with someone else or even alone, I am Yours."

She tapped the email tab and reread Myles's letter one more time before poising her fingers on the keyboard.

Dear Myles…

Myles stared at the ceiling for an hour at least, unable to sleep. He'd typed a dozen different letters to Adriana and deleted them all until he'd been left with a bare-bones note about the field trip.

What if he'd imagined a connection? She was way more outgoing than he was. What if she were simply a curious person, focusing intently on each person who crossed her path? That could be. There hadn't been anything solid he could put a finger on. She seemed to watch him. Maybe she was wondering why he watched her.

He rolled over and thumped his pillow with a groan. That was probably all it was. He was reading far too much into her helpfulness in class. He needed to remember the first time they'd met. How pushy she'd been. The gardening module was a really big deal to her. She'd gotten her way and was making sure he was on the straight-and-narrow before she unvolunteered.

Ping.

Myles grabbed his phone, thumbed it on, and tapped the email icon. His heart skipped a beat when her email address registered.

Dear Myles,

The Palmer Pumpkin Patch sounds like an excellent idea. I clicked on the link, and it looks like they are dedicated to making it a great experience for the kids with the hay ride and all. I'm sure Violet and her friends will have a terrific time. Sam will be jealous!

He inhaled. Exhaled. So far, so good.

My parents grew pumpkins commercially when my sister and I were young. That was near Arcadia Valley in Idaho, where they still live. They also grew a corn maze to attract school groups and families. Lots of good memories, and I'm

75

happy that Violet will get a chance to enjoy the experience.

Where did you grow up?

Best, Adriana

She'd offered a tiny bit of information about herself and asked a personal question. It wasn't strictly business. Of course, it could still be random curiosity. It wasn't like she'd offered her undying love or anything like that.

Myles snorted softly. Way to jump ahead. Rome wasn't built in a day, and he'd learned that a garden wasn't harvested the day it was planted. And then there was the whole her-daughter-was-in-his-class thing. He scrubbed his hand through his hair. This was going to be a long game. A slow game.

One he might not win.

He bit his lip. He certainly wouldn't win if he didn't play.

Dear Adriana,

How interesting it must have been, growing up on a pumpkin farm! I bet you know a thousand and one recipes to make use of that ingredient.

He started to delete the sentence, but left it in. For someone who made his living standing in front of twenty-five children and talking, tapping in a response to this email seemed an impossible task. So much was on the line.

I grew up in Pullman, middle of three boys in four years. My parents were both on staff at Washington State University. They split up when I was in high school, and I spent as much time as I could with my dad across the state line in Moscow, Idaho, after that. My mom had a few rosebushes in the front yard, but that was the extent of the gardening. The farmers market in Moscow is pretty cool, though. Ever been?

Too much information? Not enough? How should he know? He'd never put himself forward to get to know a woman like this before. He didn't want to come across as desperate. Best to close it right there. He signed off and hit send before he could second guess himself into deleting the entire email.

Myles clicked his phone off and lay it on the nightstand before stretching out on his bed, arms behind his head. Sleep was so far away he might as well exchange his sleep pants for gym shorts and pump some iron in the bedroom next to his. He flung the blanket aside and sat up.

"God? I'm feeling really unsure of what steps to take here." If any. That was the cruncher, wasn't it?

Ping.

He paused in mid-reach and stared at his phone before grabbing it up and checking who the email was from. His heart lurched. Adriana.

Dear Myles,

I've never been to the Moscow Farmers Market, though I've heard it's terrific. I'd like to check it out sometime. Have you ever been to the Night Market in Kendall Yards across the river? It's closed now for the season but, if you haven't been, you should check it out come spring.

My sister is six years younger than I am, so we weren't close growing up. She's turned into an amazing adult, and we're trying to get to know each other now. The kids enjoy Skyping with her. She teaches preschool in Nampa. Incidentally, that's where my parents took Violet and Sam to the rodeo, and Violet became entranced with mutton busting, like she told you at that first parent-teacher meeting.

Myles remembered the belligerent set of the little girl's jaw and the defiant expression on her face. It had matched her mom's, but Adriana's had softened. Violet was still hands-down the most difficult child in his classroom. Every day he struggled to find a new way to engage her in learning and to draw her out. She was a challenge, but he was up for it.

If he were going to pursue any woman with a child in his class — which was an exceptionally bad idea to start with — he should pick someone whose child was sweet and intent on learning. Yeah. Logic was failing him double time.

What was it like growing up at a college?

Best, Adriana

Before he made a conscious decision, he'd tapped the reply icon. There might be no logic, but sometimes a man had to pursue the opportunity in front of him... with all due circumspection. How else would he know what might have been?

Chapter 9

ADRIANA SWUNG OFF THE YELLOW school bus behind Juanita Ramirez on an overcast October day. At least she and Catalina weren't the only parent chaperones today. Sky's mom never seemed to miss a glance between Adriana and Myles… and that was before the email exchanges had begun a few days ago. Now she didn't so much as dare to peek his direction.

Myles sorted the children into groups as they dismounted the bus, placing both Violet and Sky in Juanita's group.

Violet folded her arms across her chest. "But I want to be with Sabrina."

"Not today." Myles smiled at the girl.

Adriana held her breath. Her daughter would either throw a hissy fit or concede. Until it happened, there was no way to know which way it would swing and if the tantrum won, Myles would have to deal with it. Violet had been increasingly difficult at home the past few days. How could Myles write such sweet words to the mother of his wild-card student? Not that he'd declared undying love or anything like that. The ongoing exchange, now partially shifted to texting, was simply two adults getting to know each other as though they lived in different towns. It wasn't like they could get a coffee and talk in Bridgeview Bakery and Bistro. Not with the eyes of the entire community trained upon them. Judging them.

Catalina mumbled something under her breath about a spoiled brat.

"Come on, Violet." Juanita held out her hand. "We'll have more fun than they will, anyway. We're first in the corn maze."

Violet looked between the adults. "But…"

No looking at Myles. No looking at Violet. No looking at Catalina, though Adriana could be thankful Sky wasn't in her own group today.

Juanita leaned down and whispered something in Violet's ear.

The little girl sent one more glower to her audience then tucked her hand in Juanita's.

Adriana dared breathe as she lined up her group. *Lord, what am I going to do with my daughter? She's never been easy, but she seems to be reaching for new heights of obstinacy these days. How can I get through to her? Because, right now, I'm terrified of puberty.*

Whew, that was still a few years away. Surely God would send an answer before then. It wasn't for lack of praying or seeking solutions. It wasn't for lack of standing up to her child. She'd had Violet tested, but no disorders were evident. Maybe she should hire Rebekah for some one-on-one counseling sessions. Or maybe she and Sam needed counseling, too. Who knew?

"Ms. Diaz?"

She blinked at Myles's formal address and nearly lost herself again, this time in his deep blue eyes. "Yes, Mr.

Sheridan?" Talk about playing a double game.

"Your group is first on the hay ride. Mr. Palmer is ready for you." He pointed to where a pair of huge horses stood hitched to a wagon loaded with bales.

"Okay." She tore her gaze from his and led her half dozen children to the wagon then stood by the makeshift steps and helped the littlest ones to climb inside.

"Everyone ready?" the farmer called.

The children chorused their agreement, and he flicked the reins over the horses' backs. The wagon lurched into motion.

Mr. Palmer launched into a rendition of the pumpkin song and soon had the children singing along as they headed out to the field where at least a dozen varieties of squash grew amid large green leaves. He told them about the Cinderella pumpkins, the white pumpkins, and the bluey-gray pumpkins. Soon he let the children off the wagon to select the ones they wanted to take home. After everyone had a chance to explore, Adriana marked each child's initials on the bottom of his or her choice with a felt-tip pen.

In what seemed like no time, the wagon carried them back to the main farm yard where Catalina's group waited to take their place.

After the corn maze and then story time, they headed to the picnic area for their sack lunches. The other groups joined them as they completed their own third adventure. Adriana watched Violet and sighed in relief. It seemed her daughter had settled down and was enjoying the day. Now she sat with Sabrina and Desiree as they dug into their sandwiches, chattering a mile a minute about the adventures they'd had and what they still looked forward to.

Adriana took her sack lunch over to where Juanita sat on the edge of the group. "May I join you?"

Her friend scooted over, smiling. "Sure. Seems I hardly ever get to see you these days."

Adriana sighed. "I know. It's been so busy. I've finally sewn and hung all the draperies for the Ridleys. They have a huge house, so a lot of windows needed covering."

"Helps the bank account, too, doesn't it?"

"Sure does. I haven't even had time to think about starting the home-restaurant idea, and now seems like a weird time to do it when there isn't much fresh produce available."

"Other than pumpkins."

Adriana chuckled. "Right."

"We should have a teacher appreciation night. Would you like to cater that if we did it? I was thinking of bringing the idea up at the next PTA meeting."

Adriana had taken the year off the parent-teacher association. Her eyes found Myles clear across the picnic area with Sky and Catalina next to him. She wasn't worried about how he felt about the other mom. Not after the email exchange had turned somewhat personal. "I don't think it would be a good idea for me to host."

Juanita's brows rose. "Why on earth not? It seems right up your alley."

"Um. Normally, it would be. Not this year."

"There's something you're not telling me."

Just then Myles looked up and met Adriana's gaze for a long moment. Even across the space she could feel the warmth in his eyes as his lips lifted just a little inside his beard and mustache.

"Oh."

Adriana looked at her friend. "Pardon me?"

"Did I just notice something?"

She turned, straddling the picnic bench, her back to

Myles. "What do you mean?"

Juanita leaned a little closer and whispered, "Is there something going on between you and our new teacher?"

Define *going on*? "Not really?" After all, they'd been extremely cautious, neither admitting the attraction.

"You know lying is a sin, right?"

Trust the pastor's wife to point that out. A quick glance around revealed no one near enough to overhear so long as she kept her voice down. "This isn't a good time to talk about it."

Juanita's eyes glimmered. "So there *is* something?"

"Would you ladies like a donut?" A young woman held a tray in front of her. "Fresh made this morning and drizzled with a pumpkin glaze."

"They look great." Adriana helped herself. "Thanks."

"I'm not leaving this topic," Juanita whispered as the server moved on.

"For now, you need to."

The field trip had been a success. Myles heaved a sigh of relief as the groups gathered back at the farmyard before boarding the bus.

"Oh, you'll want your picture taken, too." Juanita Ramirez stood beside his elbow.

He glanced over to the painted cut-outs where Adriana snapped photos of children peeking out from circles in scarecrows, farm animals, and corn stalks.

"Did you get my picture?" shouted Desiree.

"How about mine?" called Sky.

Adriana laughed as she thumbed on her phone. "I'll send these to your parents, okay? Anyone else?"

Myles strolled closer. It was like he couldn't help himself. "I'd love copies, too. We could decorate the big bulletin board in the classroom with memories of today."

"Sure." She didn't look at him. "Then you need to be in one as well. What's your pick? Scarecrow? Jack-o'-lantern?"

"I, uh… really?"

"For the bulletin board."

"Maybe the rooster," commented Juanita, eyes dancing. "What do you kids think? Where should Mr. Sheridan get his picture taken?"

"The rooster would be funny!" called Desiree.

"Rooster!" chorused a few others.

He held up his hands in mock defeat. "The rooster it is." He knelt behind the cut-out, which had been built at kid height, not adult, and grinned at Adriana as she snapped the shot.

"I think it's your turn." He gestured to Juanita and Catalina as he held out his hand for Adriana's phone. "All of you parent helpers would make great corn stalks."

The women chuckled and posed while he took several photos, a few quick shots zoomed in of Adriana. He'd email her later and ask her for copies. No one else needed to know.

He looked around at the students. "Anyone else? No? Then it's time to thank Mr. Palmer for the great day and the scrumptious donuts before you climb on the bus. Don't forget your pumpkin."

The children called out their thanks. A few little girls even ran over and hugged the farmer. Soon the bus was loaded and pulling out of the parking lot and back toward Bridgeview.

"Can I see those pictures?" he heard Catalina say from the back of the bus.

His blood chilled.

"Sure," Adriana replied. "Feel free to email yourself any that you want."

No. But Adriana didn't know she'd been the star attraction in the last several. He closed his eyes and waited.

"Well, isn't that interesting!"

If anyone would find it so, it would be Catalina Romero.

"What do you mean?" Adriana leaned over the seat to look over Catalina's shoulder.

Sky's mom held the phone just out of Adriana's reach, but tipped toward her. "Just this." She swiped back through five close-ups of Adriana before the group pictures began. She turned toward Adriana with eyebrows raised. "I hardly think that's appropriate."

"It's my phone." She didn't need to ask who had taken those or when. The evidence was pretty clear.

"I wonder why Mr. Sheridan didn't take *my* picture by myself? Or maybe Juanita?"

"I can't answer that question." Scratch that. She absolutely could, but didn't feel the need to.

From a few seats nearer the front, Juanita watched, eyes wide. From up at the front, Myles's face blanched and his eyes closed, not looking at her. The children, for the most part, where chattering and showing their pumpkins to each other. A few were paying attention. Smirking, Sky jabbed Violet across the back of her seat.

Adriana's gut tightened. "I'll take my phone back now."

"In a minute." Catalina twisted further out of reach and busily tapped.

"Catalina, it's my personal device. Please give it back." She could make a grab for it, but what good would it do? The other woman had already seen everything there was to see. And besides, she wouldn't hand it over easily. All Myles needed was two parents brawling on the bus to make the field trip complete.

"I'm sure he was just making certain I had memories of my own from this day. Like I said, it's my phone."

"Uh huh." Catalina's fingers didn't slow.

She was probably emailing herself what she considered evidence. But how could it be portrayed as such? It wasn't like Adriana and Myles were together in a photo, gazing at each other. Or kissing.

Yes, she'd like to kiss Myles. The realization leaped at her. But that wasn't going to happen. Not for a long time, if ever, thanks to people like Catalina Romero.

"Here you go." The phone smacked back into Adriana's hand. "Thank you so much. That's a great shot of Sky poking out of a pig's head."

It sounded triumphant as well as accusatory. "That's where he wanted his photo taken."

"Is it now?" Catalina's eyes glittered as she pressed a smile to her lips. "Interesting."

Adriana slid the phone into her pocket and stared out the window at the passing scenery. Why had the other woman wanted those photos? There had to be a reason. Catalina had a plan for them. All she could do was wait for the other shoe to drop. Meanwhile, there wasn't anything she could do.

She definitely couldn't ask Myles what to do next. If anyone was going to be in trouble, it would be him, even though the situation had been completely innocent.

A quick glance toward the front of the bus showed him facing forward with his head against the window. Probably praying.

That was the only thing left to do.

Chapter 10

RANDI PHILSON TURNED FROM her computer as Myles entered the office. "Come on in."

It wasn't the first time he'd darkened a principal's office door since he was a child, but this was the first time that same feeling knotted his gut. "Hi, Randi. You wanted to see me?"

"I do. Why don't you close the door and have a seat?"

He did so, then clasped his hands together as he waited. It could still be no big deal. A minor question about an aspect of his teaching.

"I had a visit this morning from Catalina Romero."

His gut sank. As he'd suspected. Dreaded. "She has this thing for me. I promise, I've done nothing to encourage her."

Randi's eyebrows rose. "That adds a new dimension to what I was about to say."

Uh oh. Catalina had shown those photos to the principal. He waited.

"She mentioned she accompanied your class to the pumpkin patch the other day. That she is one of two parent volunteers for the garden program for your classroom."

Myles nodded.

"She mentioned that she felt your behavior toward the other parent volunteer made her uncomfortable."

Myles surged to his feet. "She's the one who makes *me* uncomfortable."

Randi pointed at his vacated chair, and he resumed his seat. It was all he could do to still his jiggling knee at the accusation.

"She said it was a distraction to the children, and she feels that Violet Diaz has become the teacher's pet because of your obsession with the girl's mother, Adriana."

"Seriously? Have you even *met* Violet? She's one-hundred percent wired against being any teacher's pet. The child is rude and obnoxious."

"Let's start at the beginning." Randi arranged a stack of papers into a neat pile with edges aligned. "Adriana Diaz is one of the garden volunteers."

"She is."

"She is a single parent."

Myles nodded and bit back the words that he'd known more than one teacher who'd gone off the rails with a *married* parent. Or a married teacher with a single parent. But he wasn't off the rails. Not even close.

"She's pretty much teaching your class, according to Ms. Romero."

As though parent volunteers hadn't been used in that capacity before, in other times and places. "She is a gardening expert. I'm not even a beginner."

"Are you romantically involved with Adriana Diaz?"

89

Define romantically involved? Sure, she'd caught his eye, but he hadn't done anything about it besides snap a few photos of her on her own phone. That was nothing. Nothing at all compared with what he wanted to do. Realization swept him. If he'd let himself go, he'd have invited her on half a dozen dates by now and spent time kissing her on the doorstep.

"Myles? Simple question. Yes or no."

"Not a simple question." He met Randi's gaze. "I do feel a spark when she's around, but I wouldn't jeopardize my job to follow through on an impulse like that." His heart sank. The emails he and Adriana had exchanged were from his personal email address. There was no reason to disclose them. Besides, there was no incriminating evidence in them.

He'd worked hard to avoid acknowledging the depth of his interest, even to himself. After all, if he didn't admit to himself that it was real, he didn't have to think about the consequences. But with that realization came the reminder that the end of the school year was over seven months away. Only when Violet was no longer his student would pursuing Adriana not be a conflict of interest.

"Ms. Romero told me you were taking photos of Ms. Diaz on the field trip."

Photos he hadn't seen yet. "It was on Adriana's phone. She'd been taking photos of the students, and I offered to take some of the chaperones."

"And of her alone."

"It was her personal phone. I thought she'd like the memory."

"So Ms. Romero is making up a connection?"

Myles shoved his hand through his hair. "Not exactly. But I'd swear on a stack of Bibles that I haven't done or said anything remotely inappropriate. And I'm a Christian man, Randi. I don't make that statement lightly."

She nodded. "I think it would be best if Ms. Diaz no longer volunteered with your classroom."

"Only if you can prevent Ms. Romero from doing the same."

The first hint of a smile creased Randi's face. "That I can do, but only if you assure me you can handle the gardening classes without *any* volunteers. Otherwise it gets awkward."

Myles closed his eyes and breathed a prayer. How could he manage? But he did have a bit more understanding than before Adriana had led the first class. Maybe he could sort Bianca Lopez's notes more easily based on Adriana's introduction of the subject matter.

He met the principal's even gaze. "It doesn't sound like I have much choice."

"Bridgeview Elementary is a small school in a close-knit community, Myles. I can't fire you for dating Ms. Diaz, but I do ask you not to make it so that more parents are pressuring me to do just that."

"I'm sorry for putting you in a difficult position, Randi. It was not my intention. I won't escalate the situation." *Escalate the situation?*

"Thank you, though I also know a person can't simply decide whom to fall in love with and when. I've known Ms. Diaz since Sam entered kindergarten. I like her a lot, and wish all the best for her. I'd be delighted to see her find happiness and love again. But this, with you, puts the school and me, as the principal, in a difficult spot. It's not like I can move Violet into another second grade classroom. Yours is the only one."

He nodded. He hadn't been looking for love, either.

Maybe what he felt was only a mild interest and, if he didn't see Adriana regularly, his feelings would drift away. Doubtful, but maybe. He'd find a different church to attend and focus on being the best elementary teacher — the most unbiased teacher — Bridgeview had ever hired. He could do this. He'd make himself do this.

Randi met his gaze. "I'll contact both volunteers and let them know they won't be needed anymore. That's everything then. Have a great weekend."

"Thank you." Myles rose and returned to his classroom to grab his jacket and folders. It wasn't going to be easy to set Adriana out of his mind. Not easy at all. But he had to protect his career and avoid a black mark on his teaching record.

Adriana didn't need him. She needed someone more outgoing. Someone stronger who could help her take Violet in hand.

Not him. He was the wrong man for her.

"Ms. Diaz? This is Principal Philson calling from Bridgeview Elementary."

Wow, that was formal. Adriana clenched her tattletale phone. "Yes, this is Adriana. What can I do for you?" For the first time since Sam entered kindergarten, she could wish communication from the principal meant one of her kids had been misbehaving in school, but she had a strong suspicion neither of them were the focus of this call.

"It's come to my attention that there seems to be romantic interest between you and Mr. Sheridan, the teacher of one of your children."

No beating around the bush there. "We're friends." Sure, she'd like more — maybe — but he'd said nothing to push the relationship that direction, and neither had she.

"It seems he is a friend who took photos of you on a recent field trip. A friend you've been working closely with on Tuesday afternoons in the school garden."

Catalina had forwarded the image files. Of course, she had. "I'd been taking pictures of the children and he offered to snap some of the parent volunteers."

"And he did, but there are several of you alone."

"That's hardly proof he has a romantic interest." If proof, it was very subtle.

Ms. Philson sighed. "I understand that the two of you have been circumspect and that the relationship is new and fragile. I'll be honest. I'm in an awkward position here. Ms. Romero explained how uncomfortable the situation has made her, and so I've had to make a decision."

Catalina was uncomfortable? Yeah, right. The other woman was jealous, if anything. Why couldn't she just leave Myles alone?

"I need to ask you to cease volunteering in Mr. Sheridan's classroom. This includes the Tuesday garden class as well as any field trips for the remainder of the school year."

Adriana reeled. "But…Violet…"

"I'm sorry. For what it's worth, Ms. Romero is under the same restriction."

If that was meant to make her feel better, it failed. Well, maybe not utterly. "I don't know what to say. I've always made it a point to be an active partner in my children's education."

"And you've been a welcome volunteer. I know Ms. Bertoli will be delighted to have you continue to assist in Sam's classroom."

How could Adriana explain to Violet why she was helping out there and not in hers? There'd be an explosion. Fireworks, and not the fun Fourth of July kind. "Violet will be very disappointed. I assure you I haven't done anything to pursue a relationship with Mr. Sheridan." She paused. "Could you reconsider?"

"I'm very sorry, but my hands are tied. As I told Mr. Sheridan, I can't fire him for this situation, but I could undergo a lot of pressure to do so. Bridgeview Elementary has a reputation as a healthy learning environment, and I can't let anything interfere with that."

Randi had talked to Myles. Of course she had. She was Myles's boss. How had he responded? Had he admitted an attraction?

This was crazy. They'd exchanged a few emails. Okay, a few dozen by now. But they weren't deeply personal. They were only getting to know each other. Finding out each other's background. Likes, dislikes. Hobbies. Philosophies in life.

Discussions she and Stephan'd had over coffee and cheesecake in Morley's Café twelve years ago. Discussions she'd never had with another man before or since. She could tell herself all she wanted that they were just friends, but her heart knew. She was halfway in love with Myles Sheridan.

Adriana found her voice. "Thanks for letting me know."

"I'll tell you what else I told him. I've come to consider you a friend over the past three years, and I hope this won't change. As a friend, and not as Myles's supervisor, I think the world of you both and would be delighted if you found love with each other… but not while he's your child's teacher."

"It's not like that leaves any options."

Randi Philson chuckled. "Time is the only one. I can't transfer Myles two months into the school year, and there's no other classroom to move Violet to, either. Not that I'd recommend moving your daughter. I don't think she'd do well with that sort of change."

"I understand." Which was totally not a lie. Adriana could just imagine Violet's response to being separated from Desiree and Sabrina. To entire new routines. And if she knew it was her mother's fault…

"It's only seven months until the end of May. All I'm asking is that you place this budding romance on hold until then. And, personally, I do wish you all the best."

Only seven months? That loomed like an entire lifetime, now that she'd found someone she wanted to get to know. That she potentially wanted to share the rest of her life with. That, truth be told, she was falling in love with, as hard as she'd tried not to admit it even to herself.

"That's everything, then. I'll talk to you again soon."

"Thanks for calling, Ms. Philson." Adriana clicked the phone. Right. She should thank the principal for firing her from her daughter's classroom?

Was Myles worth it? But it didn't even matter anymore. Even denying she felt anything for him couldn't redeem the situation at this point. Pretty sure Randi Philson still wouldn't let her resume volunteering.

This was crazy. Myles was so different from Stephan. How could she find both men so attractive? Maybe the truth was that she and Myles *were* just friends. God knew she needed friends. Needed male friends to offer a masculine influence on her kids.

The fifth anniversary of Stephan's death loomed only a few days away. Her sister had told her she'd waited long enough. She'd adjusted to life without him, but just because the wrenching grief had passed didn't mean she was ready to love again.

Tell that to her traitorous heart.

Chapter 11

WHAT DO YOU MEAN, you're not planning to come to the dedication of the new community center?" Francesca stood in Myles's kitchen, hands on her hips. "You're part of Bridgeview now, and this is a huge event. We've been working toward this for months."

"I, uh…" Myles rested his hand on the back of a chair. "I have report cards to write. And class prep to do. Sorry."

"Would you miss the Fourth of July fireworks for that?"

"Well, since they're in summer, it's not an issue."

"Myles, you know what I mean. In Bridgeview, this is just as important."

"I don't really do crowds…"

Fran tilted her head and studied him. Even worse than being argued with. What was she seeing? Thinking? Analyzing? A sudden thought struck him. Had Adriana told her friend she'd been banned from helping at the school garden on account of his one impulsive moment? Although, Catalina had been looking for an incident. Sooner or later, she'd have found something else. He'd simply handed her the golden opportunity, and she'd run with it.

"I think you need to come, Myles. It's a potluck, but don't worry about that. There will be plenty of food. You met my nonna at Adriana's on your moving day. It seems she's always forgetting she's one person and cooks enough for the big family she used to have. She's not the only one who brings lots."

Marietta Santoro. Oh, yeah, Myles remembered the older woman who'd spoken her mind about male elementary teachers. It was supposed to be a recommendation for the community dinner that she'd cook an excessive amount of food? Although her green beans that night had been unbeatable.

"They'll be dedicating the new community garden right afterward. Nonna donated the land for that. My uncle Ray — his sons Basil and Alex helped you move — has been overseeing the work on it, and it's pretty cool. If you haven't stopped by yet, you really should. You might get some ideas for your school garden. Linnea Ranta's in charge there, and she's put in a butterfly garden as well as—"

"Butterfly garden? What on earth is that?"

Fran grinned. Yeah, she had him now and knew it. "Plants chosen specifically to attract butterflies. Of course, there aren't any here this time of year, and the garden is a bit sparse until spring planting, but you'll be impressed. They've set aside a space for a couple of beehives my cousin Jasmine will be in charge of."

"I think I've seen that. Next door to your grand-mother's?"

"Yes, that's the place. Linnea and Logan Dermott are doing amazing work, and you should take the chance to get a closer look." Fran brushed the words aside. "Anyway, please say you'll come. You can sit with us if you like. We're walking over, leaving in half an hour or so."

Why couldn't he have a quiet evening in his suite? All he wanted was to mull over what had happened again and try to figure out what to do next. Praying wouldn't go amiss, either — not that he'd done much all night besides think and pray. He certainly hadn't been sleeping.

"I'll send Tieri down to get you when we're ready to leave, okay?" Fran whisked out the door.

Myles rubbed his beard as she clattered up the outside steps to the carport. Had he agreed to go? He didn't remember saying the words, but somehow it seemed a decision had been made, regardless.

Adriana would be there. The Adriana he didn't dare look at for more than three seconds, let alone sit beside or talk to, which was all the reason he needed to stay home.

It was also all the reason he needed to go.

Tieri skipped beside him, chattering a mile a minute about the yummy food her parents carried, Luca tucked in a carrier on Tad's back. She'd helped her mom make a kale salad and a raspberry cake, informing him that she'd helped pick the berries.

The feast spread out on the tables in the community hall looked unlike any potluck Myles had ever been to. No tuna casseroles or deli packs of pasta salad in sight. Even the mix of aromas smelled more... real. Less commercial.

Fran ducked into the kitchen, cake in hand, while Tad made room on the food tables for the salad. "Been in here before?" he asked.

Myles shook his head as he took in the impressive interior. "It's a cool building. You said it hasn't been the community center for long?"

"No. It used to be an art gallery when I was a kid, but it

closed down ten, maybe twelve years ago now. Building sat empty for a lot of years until the community association was able to take it over. We've been renovating the place since late winter, and we're finally done."

"Great architecture. I can see why everyone wanted to save it."

"We got a grant for taking the whole building solar." Tad pointed at a large white rectangle on the brick wall beside the kitchen door. "That there's a Tesla power pack, charged from solar panels on a tower up on the roof."

Myles blinked and took in the light fixtures, the microphone on a stand with a compact soundboard nearby. Giant ceiling fans circled lazily. "Really? All solar? Even the kitchen?"

"Yep." Tad sounded smug. "Over there by the door? That guy with the curly blond hair? He's an architectural engineer and the mastermind behind it. Jacob Riehl." Tad chuckled. "Heard he finally proposed to Eden. I think that's his parents come to meet the fiancée."

The man in question looked to be younger than Myles by several years. Jacob held the hand of a woman with red-gold hair while they chatted with a middle-aged couple. Obviously, the younger man was practically a genius to have earned that degree by his age. Engaged to a pretty girl. Two parents who looked at each other and laughed with the younger couple.

A twinge of jealousy swept through Myles. Here he was, an elementary school teacher with divorced parents and the woman of his dreams unattainable. Okay, that wasn't completely true. He just had to wait a long time for her, more like the biblical Jacob than the one across the room.

But was that his own doing? Because he avoided

conflict? No, Randi Philson had set out the repercussions clearly. He had little choice but to avoid Adriana or put his career at risk.

Just then, Violet and Sam dodged past the foursome near the door, Adriana trailing behind them carrying a large casserole. She was gorgeous in a slim golden dress, her hair pulled back from her forehead with a copper clasp then cascading down her back in loose curls. Her face lit up.

Was she looking at him? His mouth dried. But, no. She leaned toward... Eden, was it?... in a hug. She beamed at the older couple and shook their hands.

All Myles wanted was to be near her. He forced his gaze away and focused on Tad's chatter beside him. He needed to keep his head in the game.

Adriana tucked her slow cooker full of taco stew into place on the long tables bowed with food. If she turned around now, she'd be looking straight at Myles. He was standing only a few yards away with Tad Amato. Sure, the room likely contained a hundred other people, but she knew herself. This group was the wrong one to notice the attraction between them. Whom was she trying to fool? There was no right audience. Randi had made that clear enough on the phone.

She ducked into the kitchen. "Anything I can do to help?"

Kass North, one of the cousins who owned Bridgeview Bakery and Bistro, glanced up from the work island and grinned. "Hi, Adriana. What did you bring? Whatever you brought is sure to be amazing, and I want to get a taste."

"Just a taco stew. It's in a black slow cooker." Adriana leaned over the island. "How about you? That looks delicious."

"This is Marietta's ravioli salad. She says she had Jasmine over hand-cranking the pasta at six this morning. I'm just mixing in the dressing as she instructed. Hailey and I brought desserts this time."

Fran popped out of the walk-in pantry off to the side. "Hi, Adriana. Isn't this kitchen great?" She spread her hands. "I hadn't had a chance see it since it was finished a couple of weeks ago."

Her friend was right. The designers had definitely managed to keep the character of the old building while ensuring the kitchen met commercial standards with stainless counters and backsplashes. Industrial appliances lined the aging brick walls. Adriana ran her hand over the curved metal edge of the island as her gaze drifted upward.

Her breath caught. Just below the open-beamed ceiling hung a row of colorful framed paintings of various fruits and vegetables done in childish strokes. A deep purple eggplant with a yellow frame sat above the pantry door. "Are these from Myles's class?"

Fran chuckled. "Tieri is so jealous, but yes. Haven't you seen Violet's before?"

Adriana shook her head. "I heard all about it, but I hadn't seen it."

Her friend edged closer and lowered her voice. "He's really trying to incorporate the whole food bit into everything the class is doing."

"I see that." How much did Fran know? Adriana gave her friend a sidelong glance. Myles wouldn't have confided in his landlady, would he? Probably not of his own free will, but

Fran had a way of weaseling information out of people.

"How are you doing?" Fran asked quietly.

About what, specifically? About Myles? Not well. The situation stank worse than the chicken coop in the heat of summer.

"Do I still have your kids tonight?"

Adriana took a deep breath. How could she have almost forgotten? Today was the fifth anniversary of Stephan's death. Fran always had Sam and Violet over for the night. They did some crafts and baking for the community Halloween party, leaving Adriana time to grieve.

Did she still need to cry her eyes out? She'd always mourn, one way or another, but the edge had softened in the past few months. She could sure use the time to pray, though, and try to figure out if God was really leading her into a relationship with Myles. To say nothing of what that meant to her memories of Stephan.

No one would fault her and say it was too soon to fall in love again. No, the blunder lay in her choice. Her *heart's* choice, as her mind had little to do with it and was still fighting the battle.

"Adriana? I'll come by after the dedication and get their overnight bag, okay? Looks like you need it."

She took a long breath and met her friend's gaze. "I could use the time, yes. There's a lot to think about. Pray about."

Fran's eyebrows rose slightly, and her eyes twinkled. "Myles?" she mouthed.

"Maybe," Adriana whispered. "But this isn't the time or the place to talk about it."

Indeed, several women had bustled through the kitchen while they'd talked.

"Come sit with us," Fran suggested, tugging at her arm.

Adriana shook her head. "I'd better not this time. I'll find a seat with Rebekah and Wade, or someone else." Not near Catalina Romero, if she were here.

"Why not?" Fran looked puzzled.

"Long story, but trust me. Wherever he is, I need to be somewhere else, and I know everyone here. He doesn't."

"You owe me a coffee and a good talk."

"Not today, okay?" Fran might be one of her closest friends, but that didn't mean she was a safe confidante. Not with Myles living under her roof.

"I'll take a raincheck."

From out in the main hall, Ray Santoro's voice came through the microphone. "If everyone would find a seat, I'll ask the blessing, and we can get started before this food gets cold."

Adriana followed Fran through the doorway, Kass behind them both. Fran edged around a few people to the chair Tad had saved for her. Adriana carefully avoided looking at Myles sitting on the other side of Tad. She spotted Violet with Sabrina Ramirez, and Juanita waved her over. A quick glance revealed a smiling Sam next to Caden, so Adriana made her way to where the pastor's family sat. "Thanks for saving me a seat," she said as she slid in next to Juanita.

"No problem. We thought you might like to be with Violet."

Would the time come when she and Myles attended an event like this with the kids, like a real family? Adriana shook her head, trying to dislodge the mental picture. Her neighbors and friends were always so good about pitching in with Sam and Violet, taking one or the other under wing. Most of the time, she felt like a family.

"Please rise," invited Ray Santoro. Chairs scraped then noise died down. "Father God, we thank You for Your many blessings to us every day. We thank You for friends and neighbors to share our lives with. We thank You for Your bounty, as represented by the food on this table." He paused. "Please join me in repeating the Lord's prayer. Our Father in heaven, hallowed be Your name…"

Adriana recited the familiar words in unison with her neighbors as the prayer they were meant to be. "Your kingdom come. Your will be done on earth as it is in heaven. Give us this day our daily bread and forgive us our debts, as we forgive our debtors. And do not lead us into temptation, but deliver us from the evil one. For Yours is the kingdom and the power and the glory forever. Amen."

Your will be done on earth as it is in heaven… lead us not into temptation… Yes. An evening — a night — to think and pray in solitude would be mighty welcome about now.

Chapter 12

*H*E COULD GET FIRED FOR THIS.

Well, maybe not fired, but he'd certainly get hauled back into Randi's office and get a stern talking to. After all, he'd agreed not to escalate the situation. Whatever he'd meant by that.

There could be more than one interpretation for what he was doing, right? No? *Nice try, Sheridan.*

Myles cycled down the quiet street without a safety vest. No reflective stripes to glow if a car's headlights shone on him. No headlight of his own to pierce the darkness.

It was utter insanity to assume he'd be welcome at Adriana's, but when Fran had mentioned why Violet and Sam were staying overnight, he'd been unable to get the thought out of his mind: she needed him.

He met no traffic as he passed dozens of houses with light flowing from the windows. Homes where families lived together, for the most part. He'd never longed for a family like he had today at the community center dedication, surrounded by his neighbors and the families of his students.

His bike fit behind the large rhododendron bush near Adriana's front door. The porch light flicked on, likely powered by a motion sensor. He took a deep breath and wiped his hands down his pants. They should be cold from the chill in the late October night air, not hot and sweaty.

Am I crazy, Lord? Should I forget this and just go back to my basement suite?

No answer came from above. The only sounds came from a distant dog barking. No vehicles, no music, no voice.

He rang the doorbell and waited. What was taking so long? This was a dumb idea. He shouldn't be here.

The door opened and Adriana stood in front of him, eyes wide. "Myles?" Duke padded up beside her.

"May I come in?" His heart pounded like crazy. He'd never in his life done anything this risky.

She stared at him for a long moment then nodded and stepped back to make room, her arms wrapped around her middle. She'd pulled her hair into a loose braid that draped over one shoulder of her baggy Gonzaga U sweatshirt. Thankfully she wore leggings, too. He hadn't even thought of the possibility she'd be in a flannel nightgown. Or worse. He hadn't thought this through at all. Still, he shrugged out of his jacket and toed off his sneakers before just standing there, staring at her, while Duke sniffed him all over.

"May I fix you a cup of tea?"

That sounded normal. Sane. He nodded. "Thanks." He followed her into the kitchen where the blinds were pulled over the windows. Whew. He slid onto a tall stool at the island.

Adriana turned on the flame under her kettle then leaned against the counter, watching him. "To what do I owe this visit? It's late, Myles. My kids aren't home, and I can easily

107

list off a dozen people who would think this was highly inappropriate."

"I know. Fran told me the significance of the date. I thought... I thought you might want someone to talk to." Or more, but he couldn't say that out loud. Not yet.

Duke circled three times and curled up into a ball beside the stainless double-door fridge. A rather large ball.

"What kind of tea would you like?"

"Whatever you prefer. I'm not picky." Not about tea, but he was certainly picky about whom he spent his time with. The rest of his life with.

She pulled a jar of dry herbs from a cupboard, set a handful into an infuser, and poured water over them into a pottery teapot. After a few minutes, she poured two cups. "Cream? Honey?"

"Yes to both."

A moment later she set both cups on the island and took the seat next to him. "Myles? You haven't said much."

Why *was* he here? Really? He turned to look at her, filling his eyes with her high cheekbones, her slanted nose, her brown eyes. Together, they formed the most beautiful face he'd ever seen. "I need to know if... if there's any chance we might... have a real relationship." He swallowed hard as she met his gaze, no flicker on her face. "If we might... fall in love. Someday." His hands tightened around the cup so forcefully he could be thankful it wasn't fragile porcelain, or he'd shatter it for sure. "Is there any hope?"

Adriana sucked in her bottom lip as her gaze roved his face. "You ask me this on the anniversary of my husband's death, knowing I'm home alone to grieve?"

He pushed the cup away, tea sloshing on the island. "I'm sorry. I don't know what I was thinking. Maybe I only imagined we were developing a connection. I shouldn't be here." He began to rise.

"Myles." Her hand covered his.

He stared at her long tapered fingers, unadorned with rings. Felt the warmth of her light clasp. Slowly he raised his gaze to hers. His mouth suddenly felt dry and his throat hoarse. "Yes?"

"Don't go."

Myles sank back onto the stool. "Are you sure? I know I was presumptuous. I-I should've asked."

"I could've left you on the doorstep. Besides, you're asking now. I'm saying, please stay. For a little while."

He turned his hand under hers. The warmth of her palm heated his as their fingers entwined. "If you're sure."

Adriana nodded. "May I tell you about Stephan?"

Her fingers tightened as he began to pull his away, not letting go.

"Okay." What else could he say? And yet, wasn't this where they had to begin? Her marriage might be over, but it was part of her. He wanted to know everything about her, and that needed to include the man she'd loved before. Maybe still loved too deeply to love again. That might be the answer she was trying to give him, too polite to simply tell him to remove himself from her kitchen and her life.

"I grew up in Arcadia Valley and came to Spokane for college. It didn't take me long to notice Stephan Diaz. He wasn't just built like a linebacker, he *was* a linebacker. Obsessed with all sports, really, and played whatever ones he could fit into his schedule. He was outgoing. Good-looking. Smart."

Smart. Myles had only that one thing in common with Adriana's late husband. He'd always prided himself on his brains. At the moment, they seemed to have failed him, though. How could he compete with the memory of a paragon like Stephan? Why was he even sitting here in this house the other man had bought for his bride?

Adriana's hand was still warm inside Myles's, though. He'd hear her story, hear the words of how she could never marry again, and make his way back to his dismal basement suite. At least he'd know and wouldn't have to wonder anymore.

"I was half in love with him before our first date in my sophomore year. I was thrilled that, of all the girls hanging onto his every word, he'd picked me. It didn't take me long to realize he was genuine to the core. He loved Jesus, volunteered with a Little League team, kept his grades up… he was the real deal."

What had Myles ever done that mattered? Sure, he had his faith. Knocking on Adriana's door against Randi Philson's express instructions was the most adventurous thing he'd ever done.

"He proposed the evening after his college graduation. I still had a year to go, but I wore that diamond proudly. I couldn't wait to be his wife."

Myles made another attempt to remove his hand, but Adriana's grip didn't lessen.

"We had a big wedding in Arcadia Valley, in my home church there. Grace Fellowship. His parents gave us the down payment for this house as a wedding gift. Stephan went to work at Fire Station Number Four, and I worked as a bookkeeper at an office downtown until Sam came along, when I shifted to part-time work. Then after Violet, I quit altogether, content in my happy little life."

Myles could see it all. The girls in his classroom would illustrate the story with hearts, rainbows, and unicorns.

"Sure, I always worried a little when Stephan went to work. When he was called to a fire. But I was also so proud of him. He reminded me constantly that his life was in God's hands, but so was everyone's. Anyone could die at any time, from any cause."

When had Adriana shifted to encase his hand between both of hers? Even though he felt anything but a hero, he could offer a bit of comfort. His other hand joined the warm clasp on the top of the island.

"Five years ago..." She took a deep breath, her gaze flicking to the clock on the wall. "Violet had had a rough day. She took being a Terrible Two seriously, which I'm sure doesn't surprise you. I really didn't want Stephan to go to work. But he had to, you know? I'd just put the kids to bed. Violet was still screaming at me from her crib, but I'd had it. Nothing would console her. I shut the door to her bedroom, knowing she couldn't get out or harm herself in any way. She was still shrieking when the doorbell rang."

Myles searched Adriana's face, but her gaze seemed focused on their joined hands.

She bit her lip. "It was the fire chief. Stephan was already gone. The old woman he'd rescued lived for another two years before dying of a stroke. Was it a good trade? I sure didn't think so. He had so much to live for. Like me and the children."

Myles rose and disengaged his hands before standing behind her tall stool. He rubbed Adriana's shoulders, gently, and she leaned back against him. His heart surged toward the warmth of her back against his chest, and it was all he could do not to gather her close.

Was he a big chicken? Stephan would have done it. He wouldn't have let a little fear hold him back. Myles couldn't compete, but he didn't have to. The other man was gone. He'd died a hero. "I'm so sorry," Myles murmured.

"It took a solid two years before I didn't cry myself to sleep every night. Two years before I didn't see bloodshot eyes in the mirror every morning. I didn't want to go on, but Sam and Violet needed me. I didn't have any choice."

There's always a choice. But he didn't say that, because he knew what she meant. He could only imagine the depths of her despair.

"So now it's been five years. I've survived. The kids have thrived. Even Violet isn't as difficult as she was as a preschooler."

"She's doing well at school." When he could turn her stubbornness toward positive actions, anyway.

Adriana's hands covered his on her shoulders. "She likes you. All I hear is 'Mr. Sheridan this' and 'Mr. Sheridan that'."

"Really?"

She nodded against his chest.

Did he dare? Yes. He couldn't hide in fear of rejection anymore. It was why he'd risked his job and come tonight, and he couldn't waste the opportunity he'd created. Myles slid his arms around her shoulders from behind and leaned down, just a little, to press a kiss into the silky hair on the top of her head.

Her hands clutched his wrists. "Myles," she said softly.

He barely heard her over the thunder in his heart. "Yes?"

Adriana twisted on the stool, turning toward him. She fingered the collar of his shirt then raised her eyes to meet his gaze.

She wasn't saying no. She wasn't pushing him away. She wasn't telling him he was a poor substitute for Stephan.

Myles gathered her close as she rose into his embrace. She was only a few inches shorter. He'd barely need to bend to kiss her. Kissing was a big step, though. There was no going back from kissing.

Her brown eyes gazed into his, full of trust. Full of wonder.

There was no going back, regardless. "Adriana, I-I care about you. A lot. Is there any chance — any chance at all — that you might feel the same way?"

Her lips parted, riveting his attention, but he wasn't done his speech. "I know this may seem like bad timing. You're mourning your late husband, and I'm... I don't know, assuming a connection that may not be real. And then there's the whole thing about this being a bad idea according to the principal. And she's right. Of course, she's right. But I'm still here. I'll wait the school year for you, Adriana. I'm a patient man. I only need to know if—"

Adriana's mouth pressed against his, silencing him. Her hand cupped the back of his neck, and her body pressed against the length of his. Which of those caused the tingles to explode into fireworks, he had no idea. Nor did he care.

Myles clutched her close and took control of the kiss, deepening it as though he knew what he was doing. And he did know. She'd offered her permission, no, her eagerness to receive his attention. Dare he say love? Maybe not quite yet. But in that moment he knew, with absolute certainty, that if she'd have him, he'd be hers for the rest of their lives.

Chapter 13

ADRIANA CURLED UP in the shelter of Myles's arms on the sofa. Twelve-thirty at night. They'd spent two hours talking and kissing. Stephan watched from the portraits on the far wall, his smile as wide and genuine as it had ever been. Stephan had loved her intensely, but he'd known he was in a dangerous line of work. He'd known the risks. Thrived on them, honestly. And he was gone. He'd loved her enough to want her needs to be met. For the children to grow up with a loving father. He wouldn't fault her for loving again.

Was she coming to love Myles? She shifted slightly in his embrace, and his hands tightened around her waist. Loving him was a definite possibility. She turned toward him and traced his short, trim beard with her fingers. Touched his lips, and felt them curve under her touch.

His blue, blue eyes opened as he gave her a slow smile. "Thank you, Adriana."

He'd given her as much as she'd given him. She leaned in to brush her lips over his. "Backatcha." This was how many of the intense kisses had started. With wonder that they'd found each other. Found each other acceptable. And more.

His hand caressed her shoulder. "Where do we go from here, sweetheart?"

Could she handle seven months of stolen moments, hoping no one found out? What if Randi Philson heard? If Catalina Romero caught Myles leaving her house? What if the children were unhappy with the thought of the school teacher replacing their hero father? What if Violet got teased at school?

She'd pushed those thoughts aside for two hours. Now they flooded her mind, pointing and dancing in ugly glee.

Adriana tried to straighten out of Myles's arms, but he didn't let go. "I don't know." She should have thought about it more before stepping aside and letting him enter her house. She should have thought long enough to send him home.

She hadn't. And she was having a hard time summoning any regrets.

"There isn't any class I can transfer to at Bridgeview Elementary. Should I look in other area schools?"

"Do teachers do that?" She loved touching the soft hair on his cheeks, feeling the short scruff as she cradled his face between her hands. "I've never seen a teacher transfer in or out during a school year, unless they were taking a leave of absence for health reasons or something like that."

"Maybe I should ask for leave."

She shook her head. "You can't do that. You'd go stir crazy without a job."

Myles shook his head, staring past her shoulder. "I'd be out on the street, too. I kind of need a job to keep paying rent."

If they married quickly, rent wouldn't be a problem. He

could move in here. A warning bell clanged deep in her mind. Of all the reasons to have a hasty courtship, that was among the worst. They'd regret it for sure.

"Maybe I could tutor."

"Do you *want* to tutor instead of teach?" The look on his face when his gaze met hers answered that question. "And it would take a while to find clients, wouldn't it? Any other options? There isn't any other second grade class to shift Violet to. Not in Bridgeview."

"And you know she'd hate being shuffled." Myles answered so quickly she knew he'd thought of that already. "We want her on board, not angry. Not feeling like she's the one who has to make all the sacrifices."

"It's not a possibility anyway."

"No, not a real one. I mean, she's bright. In theory, she could move to Natasha's classroom, but adding one second grader to the mix would eat too much of Natasha's time."

"To say nothing of separating Violet from all her friends and putting her in with her brother."

"I know it's not an option. It's just… something I thought of and discarded as quickly. But maybe by putting all the possibilities on the table, regardless of how unlikely they are, we'll think of a solution that works."

"There is one way." She brushed her lips against his, and he captured them for a longer kiss.

When they pulled apart again, he asked, "What's that?" His eyes were bright as they held hers.

Adriana took a deep breath. "We pretend tonight didn't happen, and we wait seven months."

He held her close. "I don't like your solution."

"I'm not very fond of it myself."

Myles's lips roved her face from her chin to her eyelids

to her temples before settling on her lips. She clung to him as a drowning woman clutching a life preserver in the middle of a surging river. Seven months had never seemed longer. Not even when she found out she was pregnant with Sam. Then at least she and Stephan could tell everyone. They could prepare a room for the baby and anticipate his arrival with all the fanfare the event deserved.

Hiding the fact that she was falling in love with Myles for so long seemed much more difficult. What if he moved on and found someone else in that amount of time? She knew *she* wouldn't — not after five years of mourning Stephan — but what about him?

Myles rested his forehead against hers. "Is there no other way?"

"If you can think of something, I'm all ears. Now that I've found you, I don't want to pretend I don't know you."

He quirked a grin. "I hear you. I want to shout it from the Maple Street Bridge. Take the microphone at the community center. Announce it in a school assembly. I don't want to feel like a kid sneaking around behind his parents' backs, like I'm doing something wrong. I'm thirty-two years old."

"Younger than me," she murmured.

"Is that okay? I didn't even think—"

She kissed him. "Myles. You think too much. I'm thirty-four. That's not so much. Two years makes a difference in high school. Maybe even in college. But certainly not now."

"You're sure?"

"How can you be worried about that, with all the other stuff?"

"I'm not. Not really. I just want to be certain." His hand traced her jaw.

"Sometimes you have to take a risk."

117

"Then let's just announce to everyone that we're dating. I mean, if we are." He looked at her, eyes worried and brows raised.

"If we can date without dating, that's what we're doing."

"I like to see where I'm going. I guess that's an issue for me. I don't like the feeling of walking a tightrope in the fog."

"We get a lot of mist here, along the river." Adriana nodded toward the windows overlooking the backyard. "I've learned that the mist doesn't change anything. The chicken coop is still where it was when the sun shone brightly. The garden beds, the plum trees, the river. None of it changes, even if I can't see it."

A small grin played at his mouth. "You're talking about faith. The substance of things hoped for, the evidence of things not seen."

"I guess I am. I hadn't thought of it that way before." She chuckled and angled her head. "Have you prayed about… us? For God's will to be made clear?"

He kissed her lightly. "Every day for weeks."

She had to know. "How many weeks?"

"Promise you won't laugh."

"Why would I? It's a serious question."

"Since the day I moved in at Amatos and you had the dinner here for all Fran's cousins."

Adriana's eyebrows rose before she could control them. "That long? That's almost two months."

"I know it's crazy, but it's true."

"That was just a week or so after we first met." She bit her lip. "I was kind of mean to you that day. Like a bully."

Myles's fingers slid through her hair, the braid undone long before. "Not like a bully. Like a mama bear protecting her young. I respect that."

118

She shivered at his gentle touch. "I'm sorry."

"No need." He shook his head and swept her lips with his own.

Adriana held his face in place for a longer kiss. It was easier, and maybe more full of proof, than words.

"Oh, Adriana," he groaned. "Seven months? Really?"

"Maybe I could move to Arcadia Valley for the rest of the school year. My parents have often begged me to come back, especially the first year or two after Stephan died. You could come on weekends."

"How far is it?"

She sighed. "An eight or nine hour drive."

"In summer. We're talking over the winter. It's too far, sweetheart. And it would be so hard on both children."

He was right. That long a drive would leave them barely any time to be together. The kids would hate it, plus it would disrupt the bookkeeping she did for several local businesses and the decorating clients she was working with. "It was just an idea. I didn't say it was a good one."

"What are your plans for Thanksgiving?"

"I usually stay right here. Sometimes my parents and sister visit, but not this year."

"I'm planning on going to Pullman to see my parents and my brothers." He hesitated, searching her face. "Want to come? I always stay at my dad's across the state line in Moscow, but I'm sure my mom would be happy to put you and Violet and Sam up. They'd all like to meet you. Uh, not that I've told them anything. Yet."

"Myles?"

He kissed her. "Yes?"

"If we're going to make this work, I don't think Sam and Violet can know anything is going on."

"Not—" He touched her face as evidence of his thought processes rampaged across his. "They'd never keep it a secret, would they." It wasn't a question.

"I don't think it's fair to ask them to. It would affect how they treat you at school. If they let anything slip — especially Violet — things will be very difficult there. For her. For you."

Myles surged off the sofa and strode over to the window, his hands driving through his hair. "I don't want secrets."

Her heart cracked. "I don't, either. I just don't see any other way to get through the next few months."

He pivoted, looking at her. "No dates. No dinners. No phone calls. Nothing."

"No phone calls when the kids are up, anyway." Chilled, she rose and wrapped her arms around herself. "If you have better ideas, I'm all for hearing them, but I think we've discussed every angle. I leave town, you leave town or switch jobs, we keep it a secret, or we tell everyone and let the chips fall where they may. It feels like forever now, but it will pass quickly."

She was lying, even to herself. It would feel like an eternity, seeing the man she was coming to love only from a distance, pretending he meant no more to her than any other unattached man she knew, like Peter Santoro or Dave Ranta, Junior. How could they possibly pull this off? The emails in the past couple of weeks had been great, but for that to be all they had for seven months was unthinkable. Not when she saw him nearly every day.

Not when her heart had finally admitted to its feelings.

Myles crossed the space and set his hands on her hips. "I was never very good at treading water."

She tried for a smile. "You told me you loved to swim."

"I do. I don't like working to stay in one place. And it will be work."

"Maybe… once in a while, I can ask Francesca or Juanita to keep the kids for a few hours."

His eyes brightened. "A date? But what if we're seen? One thing I've learned about Bridgeview is everybody knows somebody who knows too much."

She chuckled as she straightened his shirt collar she'd mussed while they cuddled. "So true."

"Can you come to Pullman for Thanksgiving? Without the children?" Even as he said the words, his head shook from side to side. "I'm sorry I asked."

"I can't do that to them. Not for a whole weekend. But maybe I could drive down for a few hours on Saturday. It's far enough from Spokane that we shouldn't run into anyone we know."

Myles's hands slid around to her back, tugging her that half step closer. "Please come?"

Adriana clutched the front of his shirt. "It will mean telling Fran and Tad. The fewer people the better, but I think we can trust them."

"They seem like the logical choice, if your children like going to their house."

"Sam gets bored, but Tad has lots of video games and has been known to take Sam to a football or hockey game from time to time. Tieri worships the ground Violet walks on and doesn't mind being bossed around. It seems to work."

"Fran has made a few comments about you to me." Myles stroked her back. "I think she'd be a good ally."

Adriana chuckled. "She's made more than a few comments to me. She can get downright pushy. You'd think she was related to Marietta or something." Why did it feel more manageable if they allowed one other couple inside their secret? There'd be an accountability factor, too. That might be wise. "It's one-thirty, Myles."

"Are you kicking me out?" One arm slid up to cradle her shoulders while the other encircled her waist.

She didn't want to. Not at all. But a misstep that huge was not how to begin a godly relationship. "Soon. But maybe not yet." She tugged his head down those few inches and kissed him as deeply as she dared.

Chapter 14

MYLES PACED HIS MOM'S living room. He hadn't felt comfortable in this house since Dad moved out when Myles was fourteen. His brothers both had their laptops out as they sat side-by-side on the sofa. Lance showed Keith the game his company had released yesterday on Black Friday.

Mom watched Myles. "She'll be fine. They've got the highways cleared from yesterday's storm."

"I know." There'd been a few inches, less than had been forecasted. He had no reason to distrust Adriana's driving skill, or anything about her. Introducing her to this lot consumed all his panic.

"Can't believe you've invited a girl home." Lance looked up from the computer, so much like Myles it seemed like looking in the mirror. At least if Myles let his hair grow to the shoulders and shaved his face. "What's this, your first ever girlfriend?"

At least he didn't have a flavor of the month like his younger brother. Okay, maybe more like flavor of the year, but still, Lance was one for the ladies, not one for settling down. They might look alike, but their personalities were poles apart.

"Still think it's weird that you're dating a widow with kids." Keith's fingers sped over his keyboard, and he didn't look up.

"It's too bad she couldn't bring the children today," Mom added.

Myles had explained why yesterday. Explained about the 'not dating' part. Keith and Lance had shook their heads and glanced at each other. Lance might be a player, but Keith's second marriage had landed on the rocks recently. Neither of them could understand Myles and Adriana making the choices they had.

His phone buzzed. A quick glance showed a text from Adriana. *I'm here.*

"Excuse me." He took a deep breath and grabbed his jacket.

"She's here?" Mom hurried over to the window and pulled the sheer liner aside.

Myles pushed his feet into his boots. By the time he got to Adriana's vehicle at the curb, no doubt his brothers would be watching, too. Well, let them.

Adriana swung out of her car and slid her sunglasses on top of her head. Her long brown hair flowed over her puffy parka. Her jeans-clad legs ended in tall black boots.

That was all he had time to see before he gathered her in his arms and kissed her. It had been a long four weeks since he'd last held her close. Emails and texts just hadn't cut it, but they'd given up on phone calls when Violet had overheard her mom one night and wondered who she was talking to.

Adriana's lips caressed his. "Oh, Myles. It's so good to see you. To touch you."

That was the difference, for sure. He'd *seen* her at a distance plenty of times, most days when she met Violet and Sam in the schoolyard at two-thirty, most Sundays at church, sometimes oftener. Seeing was painful when he couldn't hold. Couldn't kiss.

"We've got an audience," he murmured against her temple.

She shifted slightly to peer over his shoulder. "So I see."

"My dad is coming over soon for lunch."

"Is that good?"

"I hope so. Occasionally Mom can be civil to him. They're trying to call a truce for my sake. For yours."

Adriana touched his beard. "This is a bit scary."

He pressed his face against her hand. "For me, too. My brothers are already making a big deal of you being the first girl I've ever brought home. Not that I've exactly *brought* you, of course. But it's the closest—"

"Myles." She kissed him.

He closed his eyes. "I babble when I'm nervous."

"I've noticed. It's okay. We can do this."

"All right." He gazed into her trusting brown eyes and kissed her nose. "Can I help you with anything?"

"I'll leave the cooler in the trunk until we're ready for dessert."

"What did you bring?"

"Green tea ice cream with chunks of candied ginger. I dropped off a batch to Fran with the kids, too."

"You didn't have to go to so much trouble."

"Myles, food is my thing. You should know that by now."

He did know. "Thanks. It should be cold enough out here, right?"

Adriana nodded. "It's packed in plenty of ice, besides." She reached into her car, grabbed her purse, then shut the door and beeped it before interlacing her fingers with his. "Okay, then. Ready?"

"Ready."

They strolled up the shoveled walk then he opened the front door for her to precede him. She leaned against him for just an instant before stepping through. If she'd meant to gather strength from him, she'd also offered it.

"You must be Adriana." Mom scurried close, arms wide.

Adriana kissed the air on both sides of Mom's cheeks. "Thanks for having me."

"Oh, it's my pleasure. I'm Myles's mom, Sharon. These are my other sons, Keith and Lance."

Huh. His brothers had actually put the game on hold long enough to satisfy their curiosity.

"I'm Keith, Myles's big brother."

"Pleased to meet you."

Myles slid Adriana's coat from her shoulders and hung it in the closet. "Keith teaches geology here at WSU."

"Go Cougars," both brothers said, bumping fists.

"And I'm Lance, the fun younger brother." Lance winked at Adriana.

"Nice to meet you both."

"I was hoping you'd be able to bring your children, after all." Mom looked between them, eyebrows raised.

"It wasn't possible this time." Adriana smiled at Mom. "There will be another chance for you to meet them, I'm sure."

It wasn't like Myles hadn't explained why Adriana was

coming alone. His brothers had rolled their eyes while shaking their heads at each other. Whatever. It wasn't one of *their* jobs on the line.

Besides, looking at his family in a semi-circle in front of them, all watching — it was just as well not to inflict this on the children first thing.

"Lovely home you have here," Adriana said to his mom, looking around.

Myles hid a smirk. This house was modest compared to Adriana's. His sweetheart was not only the perfect hostess, but the perfect guest. If only he wouldn't be the one to mess everything up.

Later, Adriana and Myles walked hand in hand in Reany Park, finally away from the curious inspection.

"That went better than I expected," he said. "Your ice cream was a big hit."

"That's why I brought it." Adriana bumped his arm. "Your family is lovely. You had me terrified." Sure, it had felt weird. Weirder than the day she'd first met Stephan's parents. There'd been nothing in their way back then, just two college kids who'd toppled into love. She needed to tell them about Myles before they heard it from another source, but maybe they didn't need the information just yet? Definitely before the news broke publicly, though.

"No one has ever called my family lovely before. Didn't you see the way Mom glowered at Dad all through lunch? And, considering my brothers are in their thirties, you'd think they could talk about something other than video games."

"But Lance helped develop Sam's favorite game! I can't wait to tell him… oh." Everything was 'oh.' This skulking around was getting old, even in one month. *Only six to go.* Yeah, not much of a solace.

She'd told Fran over lunch and swore her and Tad to secrecy. She'd told her parents and her sister, Alaina, calling in the daytime, but couldn't talk freely with them on the phone other times of day for the same reason she couldn't talk to Myles — little ears that never seemed to be asleep when they should be. Besides, there was little to tell with everything on hold, other than the emails, which zinged back and forth daily.

"Penny for your thoughts?" Myles asked quietly.

Adriana shook her head. "Not worth it. I can't believe I'm wasting time worrying about things when we finally have a couple of hours together. Let's go do something."

"Violet and Sam would enjoy the Palouse Discovery Science Center. We should take them there when they come to meet my parents."

When would that be? June? Forever away. "Sounds good."

Adriana turned to Myles and slipped her arms around his bulky parka. It was much too cold to take them off and get closer — too cold to stay in the park for long, really — yet how else were they to get some time alone?

He reached between them, unzipped his coat, and wrapped the front flaps around her, nestling her against the soft sweater that covered his flannel shirt.

This was better. At least she could feel his warmth. Hear his heartbeat. Drink in the scent of his cologne. "Myles…" she murmured, closing her eyes.

He kissed her hair. "I love you."

Adriana hadn't expected to hear those whispered words just yet, but the warmth of them flowed into the chilled places in her soul. "I love you, too." She tipped her face to his.

"I've missed you so much." Myles trailed feather-light kisses across her cheeks.

She quivered at the sensation. "I missed you more."

"You'll have a hard time proving that." His blue eyes warmed as his lips tilted into a smile. "But you're welcome to try."

Two hours later, Adriana kissed Myles goodbye and pulled away from the curb. She tapped her sister's number on the Bluetooth dashboard display.

"Hey, Ads, how did it go?"

Adriana turned the car north on the highway.

"Adriana? You there? Spill everything."

"I'm in love."

Alaina's squeal reverberated through the car. "I'm so happy for you! I can't wait to meet him. Are you bringing him home for Christmas?"

"You already know why I can't do that."

"You can't seriously wait until the end of the school year to make the next move. The next official move, I mean."

Adriana took a deep breath. "No matter how many times Myles and I discuss it, we can't come up with another option. I can't ask him to put his job on the line for us."

"Why not? There are other schools in other cities. Or you guys could move back to Idaho."

"We're settled in Bridgeview. The house is paid for. I have jobs. The kids have friends. Activities. A routine."

"Sis, marrying Myles is going to disrupt your routine. It's not like you can add him like a teaspoon of sugar and make life ten percent sweeter."

Adriana gripped the steering wheel. Was that what she was trying to do? Add him to her perfectly ordered life and hope he fit into the role she offered? "The children have already lost their father. I don't think—"

"Listen to yourself," Alaina suggested. "Your kids are resilient. Don't you think they'll hate that you kept it from them for an entire year?"

"It's not a year. It's only half a year now." No one needed to remind her how long it was. The weeks since they'd admitted their feelings had crawled by painfully.

"Let me put it this way. If he wasn't Violet's teacher and you weren't terrified of him getting fired, what would be happening about now?"

"We'd be dating, probably a couple of times a week." Maybe talking about the future.

"He'd be at your house, helping the kids with their homework, taking Sam to football games."

The picture was too much. Adriana wiped a tear from her cheek, hoping her mascara wouldn't smudge. "I want that."

"Then figure out what you have to do to get it. You're thirty-four years old, Adriana. If this is the man for you, don't put him on hold. Grab him and go for it."

"Easy for you to say. I don't see you grabbing Garth and *going for* it."

There was silence for long enough that Adriana glanced at the dashboard to see if she'd lost signal. Nope. Four bars. "Alaina?"

"I broke up with him a few days ago."

"You... what? Why?"

"He had another girlfriend in Boise."

"No way."

"My friend saw them coming out of a movie. She snapped a couple of photos on her phone then switched to video mode. They kissed, Adriana. At length. I'm not sure how to misinterpret that."

"You confronted him?"

Alaina's sardonic chuckle came over the line. "And he denied it, at least until I pulled the photos up on my phone and showed him. Then he looked a bit sheepish and shrugged."

"I'm so sorry."

"Yeah, me too. I thought we had a good thing going. I guess it's better to find out before we tied the knot than after."

"True. But I hurt for you."

Alaina sighed. "It's time for a fresh start for me. I need out of Nampa. Mom tells me Grace Fellowship is opening a summer daycare in June, and a preschool and after-school program in August. As soon as they're accepting resumes, I'm applying."

"Whoa. Never thought you'd move back to Arcadia Valley."

"It's not a done deal. They might pick someone else. But seriously, I'm done with my current life. If that job doesn't pan out, I'll find something else. Maybe I'll move to Spokane."

"I'd love that. So would the kids."

"I'd come and kick your butt to tell that man you love him and will make any sacrifice so you can be together.

Which gives me an idea. Why don't you homeschool Violet?"

Horror chilled Adriana from her heart out. "Are you kidding me? Have you met my child? That's the worst punishment I could come up with." For both of them.

"I doubt it. She'd probably love some one-on-one attention, especially if she got a stepdad out of the deal."

"You're crazy. That would never work."

"Because you've thought it all through and made a decision? Live dangerously, Adriana."

"No, I haven't thought of homeschooling at all." Not once, in an entire month of longing for Myles, had the idea even poked at the fringes of her mind. She even knew some families who seemed to thrive on it, and it still hadn't registered. But she hadn't been kidding about Violet's personality. "It wouldn't work."

"Sis? Don't just knee-jerk it. Think about it. Pray about it. Because if Myles is half as great as you've told me, you need to make things work sooner rather than later."

Adriana shook her head, not that Alaina could see. "Whatever. Sure."

It was still a terrible idea. Wasn't it?

Chapter 15

ADRIANA GLANCED UP AS Rebekah deftly transferred sugar cookies to the cooling rack on the counter beside the ovens. She straightened her back and rotated her shoulders from side to side. It was going to be a long day preparing treats for the church Christmas pageant Sunday evening.

Twenty-five dozen decorated cookies. There was no way she could do this without her friends' help.

"How many shapes are we doing?" Francesca squirted pale blue gel into a bowl of royal icing and stirred.

"Some variety is fun. Once we've done the snowflakes, we'll move on to angels, Christmas trees, and then I guess we'll decide the rest."

"You'll want a darker shade of blue, too?"

Adriana nodded. She picked up her bag, checked to make sure the number two tip was attached, and outlined a snowflake in white before flooding the center. The icing evened out with a gentle tap.

Rebekah slid two more sheets into the convection oven and set the timer then turned back to roll out the next batch of dough at one end of the island. "So tell me the scoop with you and Myles. How are the garden classes coming?"

An odd squeak came from Fran as she focused intently on the color.

It had been way too long since the three of them had spent much time together. "I'm not helping in the classroom anymore." She and Myles had agreed to keep the list of people who knew what was going on extremely short, but how could she keep it from Rebekah? While they'd only known each other two years — compared to at least ten for her and Fran — Rebekah had fit in almost right away to form a trio from their duo. In fact, Rebekah had rented the basement suite from Fran and Tad back before she'd married Wade. The one Myles now lived in.

Rebekah ran the rolling pin over the thinning slab of dough. "Why not? Has he miraculously learned everything he needs to know about growing vegetables?"

"Um, not exactly, but he's doing pretty well, all things considered." Like they emailed the lesson plan back and forth to fine tune it every week. "All that snow in the past couple of weeks has effectively put the outdoor garden on hold until spring. This week Violet brought home ornaments decorated with various kinds of seeds."

"Sounds like a fun project." Rebekah narrowed her gaze at Adriana. "So how come you're not helping anymore? Did you and *Mr. Sheridan* have a fight?"

Fran choked on her snicker.

Rebekah glanced between them and pointed the rolling pin at Adriana. "Okay, what did I miss?"

Adriana took a deep breath and closed her eyes for a few seconds. "This is one hundred percent top secret, okay?"

"Okaaay."

"Randi Philson banned Adriana from the classroom," burst out Fran. "From volunteering in Violet's class at all."

Adriana felt a flush creep up her cheeks. *Thanks, Fran.* "Catalina Romero made a big deal from some things that happened on the pumpkin patch field trip in October."

"Only because that woman has a crush on Myles herself." Fran covered the bowl and reached for another color of gel.

Rebekah's eyebrows rose. "What happened?"

"On the field trip? Catalina made a mountain out of a mole hill." Adriana took a deep breath. "However, that doesn't mean she was wrong."

"Keep talking."

"Promise not to tell a soul. Or if you tell Wade, he can't tell anyone. Not one single person. I mean it. My kids don't know this, and they can't find out."

Rebekah set her hand on her heart. "Promise."

"Myles and I are dating. Or, at least, we would be, if it didn't put his job in jeopardy."

"I knew it! You guys are perfect for each other!" Just as quickly, the glee faded from Rebekah's face. "But, wow, yes, the school thing is a problem."

"Tell me about it. And the end of the school year is still over five months away." Closer than when they'd acknowledged their growing feelings after the community center dedication, but still an awfully long way away. "I can't believe a couple in their thirties in this day and age has to sneak around so no one knows they're dating."

"What kind of sneaking are we talking about here?"

Adriana glanced at Fran, who grinned widely as she created a darker blue royal icing.

"Fran kept the kids Thanksgiving Saturday, and I drove down to meet his parents in Pullman."

"So there has been mutual acknowledgment. And kissing?"

"There has been kissing." Not nearly enough of it. Although, with the length of time still looming in front of them, maybe too much.

"I'm so happy for you, Adriana. He seems like a great guy."

"He is. He really is. You know I wasn't looking for anyone to replace Stephan."

"And I told her Myles doesn't replace Stephan," Fran put in. "I mean, in some ways, yes. Like he'll be her husband one day. But her memories of Stephan are separate and real. The love is similar yet different."

Sometimes those memories seemed like they were fading into the mist, just out of focus. But Adriana couldn't live there anymore, peering into the past, trying to hold onto the wisps. The fragments would never be real again. It didn't mean she didn't love Stephan. It meant Myles was here. Real. Solid. Warm.

"And Violet and Sam don't know? That must be hard."

"I can't risk them finding out. You know how touchy Violet is about everything. She'd either be angry, which would be a challenge, or she'd gloat at school, and then she'd get teased. Either way, it's best to protect her. Sam, too, but to a lesser degree. His personality is different, plus, well, it's not his teacher we're talking about."

The timer beeped, and Rebekah exchanged trays in the wall convection oven. "Ever thought of homeschooling Violet?"

"No." She'd come up with a hundred reasons why not after her talk with Alaina. "She needs school. She needs her peers." And her mother needed time apart.

136

"Not forever. Just for what's left of this school year."

"No."

"It would mean you wouldn't have to sneak around. Isn't that worth a lot?"

That was the only thing that made the thought remotely tempting. "It isn't an option."

"Okay. I was just trying to help."

"I know." Adriana sighed. "We're adults. We'll make do with emails and texts until school's out the end of May."

"Late night phone calls…?"

"Violet came in one night when I was on the phone and wanted to know who I was talking to. She's such a restless sleeper I can't risk it again."

"Sounds like Violet rules the roost."

Frustration flared in Adriana's heart. "*You* try dealing with her twenty-four-seven. I've learned to pick my battles."

"It's not just Violet," put in Fran. "It's the school. If everyone knows Myles is in love with Adriana, they'll be watching for favoritism. You can't blame Randi Philson for trying to avert trouble."

"If Myles is in love with Adriana," Rebekah countered, "he's *already* fighting favoritism. The only difference is whether others recognize it or not."

Was that true? Did Myles treat Violet differently than the other children? Both her previous teachers had, because Violet was so strong-willed she practically demanded it. No one would think anything of extra attention. Unless they knew. No, the only answer still lay in no one finding out, especially Catalina.

"Still think homeschooling is the answer," muttered Rebekah as she arranged angel-shaped cut-outs on cookie sheets.

Yeah, well, Adriana didn't agree.

The best thing about a church Christmas pageant was that Myles could sit back and enjoy it. Bridgeview Elementary didn't host a school concert, so he was off the hook there. Myles clapped with the others after the teen group completed the final skit of the evening. The overhead lights brightened.

His gaze snapped to Adriana and her children near the front of the sanctuary as people began to rise. He belonged beside her. He wanted to give Sam a high-five for the solo he'd sung then put his arm around the boy's shoulder and tell him he was proud of him. He wanted to tell Violet what a good job she'd done as Mary. Even now the little girl's face glowed, something Myles had rarely seen. And Adriana. How he yearned to slip an arm around her and kiss her cheek like Tad had just done to Fran, even here in church.

"Hey, Myles. Haven't seen you around much." Peter Santoro leaned from the pew behind. "Coming downstairs for refreshments?"

Myles's face slid into a lopsided grin. "I wasn't planning to, thanks." There was a limit to how much torture he'd willingly put himself through.

"Aw, come on, man. You can't be part of Bridgeview without spending time with the people who live here. Let me introduce you around." He chuckled. "I know people who don't have school kids."

"I'd rather n—"

"There'll be awesome snacks. No bachelor in his right mind turns down free food."

"Well…"

Peter clapped him on the shoulder. "Come on down for a few minutes."

It was true Myles hadn't made an effort to build friendships here, not even with the guys who'd helped him move. He'd always been a loner, and this secret with Adriana made him even more cautious whom he talked to. He tipped his head. "I guess I can spare a few minutes." He followed Peter and his cousins toward the stairs.

"Myles Sheridan."

He turned slowly at the sound of Peter's grandmother's voice. "Merry Christmas, Mrs. Santoro."

She waggled a finger at him. "Marietta. We are friends, yes?"

He didn't normally make friends with personalities as forceful as this one. He'd managed to avoid her most Sunday mornings since he'd started attending here. Since she'd rampaged against him at Adriana's house that first night. Mind you, Adriana hadn't been too friendly at first, either, and look how that had turned out. Maybe Marietta was sweet under that crust, too. "Of course. How are you keeping these days?"

"My days are long with the garden put to bed for the winter. You have made a good garden at the school, Francesca tells me."

Well, look at that. An olive branch. "I'm learning along with the students. We'll start planning for next season's garden in January."

"This is good. If you need any seed catalogues I can recommend some."

"Uh… that's okay. I have sources." He counted on Adriana to keep his class pointed in the right direction, even

139

if the mentoring came in the form of late-night emails.

"If you need any advice, come visit. You will stay in Bridgeview, yes? Francesca and Marco tell me you are a good teacher, even if you are a man."

Marco? Oh, right. Another Santoro cousin who'd helped Myles out in September, the man with several young sons, one of whom was a friend of Sam's. None of the boys were in Myles's room this year. "That's kind of them to say so. Yes, I'd like to stay in this school, Lord willing."

"Every man needs a wife. How old are you? Have you met my granddaughter Jasmine?"

"Jas—" What on earth? "No, I don't think so, but that's okay. I'm really not looking." *I have found the one my soul loves*. Where in the Bible was that from, anyway? Song of Solomon. Now that was a book he ought to stay away from these days.

"Tsk. You need a woman. Jasmine is a good girl. Twenty-six. She is a massage therapist and very knowledgeable about gardens and herbs. She could help you with your project at the school."

Peter slung his arm across his grandmother's shoulders. "And Jasmine rides a Harley and will fall in love with some great guy when she's good and ready to. Quit trying to set her up, Nonna." His brown eyes gleamed as he chuckled. "Just realized you weren't behind me, Sheridan. Figured I'd come back upstairs and make sure you hadn't run off home when I wasn't looking."

Marietta patted Myles's arm. "I made struffoli. You should try some. The pan is beside that tray of beautiful cookies Adriana brought." She angled her head as she peered up at Myles. "Now there is another lovely woman who is unattached."

"Nonna…" Peter's voice held a warning.

"What, you want I should find a wife for you, Pietro? You also are of an age to marry and give me more great-grandchildren. No one heeds an old woman these days."

"You can't force love." Peter winked at Myles. "Come on, Sheridan. Half the good stuff will be gone if we don't get down there."

Indeed, the crowd in the foyer had thinned considerably, even as most of the coats remained on hangers.

"I will make you more struffoli if it is gone!" called Marietta as Myles made good his escape on Peter's heels.

"Sorry about Nonna. I guess it's a sign she's accepted you if she's trying to marry you off."

Myles managed a chuckle and followed Peter into the brightly lit basement teeming with Bridgeview residents. People everywhere, talking, laughing. Man, this was so not his scene. He hesitated in the doorway then a short body bowled into him. He staggered and caught the small shoulders. "Sam?"

The little boy looked up at him and pushed his glasses up his nose. "Hi, Mr. Sheridan."

Myles crouched to eye level. "Where were you going in such a hurry?"

"To find Caden." Sam peered past him. "Have you seen him?"

Myles shook his head. "Hey, buddy, you did a great job on that solo. Did you practice a lot?"

Sam's eyes brightened. "Yeah, every day."

Dark-tipped nails rested on Sam's other shoulder. Adriana's laugh arrowed straight for Myles's heart. "He did, though it was often against his will."

Myles raised his gaze to meet hers. "It paid off." More words fled him as he rose.

Sam shrugged away and clattered up the stairs.

Adriana took Myles's breath away in her deep red top flecked with gold. It looked soft, but a warning bell rang in his mind before he reached out to touch it. To touch her. To slide his fingers through the brown hair cascading nearly to her waist. He hadn't been this close to her since kissing her goodbye in Pullman three weeks before.

Tonight they were just two Bridgeview residents talking about a church concert. He could do this. He had little choice. "Violet did well, too."

Adriana's brown eyes shone into his. "She'd love to hear that from you."

"I'll find her." He tore his gaze away from hers and glanced around the room, looking for the little girl.

Natasha Bertoli raised her eyebrows as she looked between him and Adriana. Question marks all but bounced out of Peter's eyes. Others had turned toward them.

"Nice running into you." Myles didn't dare put any emphasis on the words. Didn't dare swim in her eyes even a moment longer.

He turned and walked away, wending his way amid the crowd, feeling like he'd chosen to dive into the Arctic Ocean rather than staying in a place of warmth and belonging.

Chapter 16

ADRIANA GLANCED IN THE rearview mirror. Sam's nose was buried in a thick tome about dinosaurs they'd checked out of the library for the holidays.

Violet bounced as much as her seatbelt would allow. "Mom?"

"Yes, sweetie?" The highway and the entire day stretched ahead of them on an overcast winter's day with no snow in the forecast until late that evening. They should be ensconced at her parents' house in Arcadia Valley before the storm hit.

"Sometimes kids say mean things."

Adriana kept her voice even. "Oh? What have they been saying?"

"Sky makes fun of me. He says Mr. Sheridan likes me best."

So Catalina hadn't gone away completely. "Why does Sky say that?"

"Some of the other kids call me teacher's pet. What is that, Mom?"

Sam shot his sister a sidelong glance. "I told you not to

143

let them talk like that."

Violet made a face at him. "Like I can stop them."

"You just tell them to be quiet and walk away. They figure it out."

How much experience did Sam have with that sort of thing, anyway? He'd been bullied a bit in first grade but had learned how to diffuse situations after Adriana had enrolled them in jiu jitsu. Violet had learned the same techniques.

"They don't listen to me." Violet glared at Sam.

"Do they say why they think that?" Adriana kept both hands on the wheel. Myles wouldn't jeopardize their relationship by treating Violet differently than the other children. Not on purpose. It would be hard to maintain neutrality day in and day out — not that anyone could treat Violet the same as any other child. She demanded so much attention.

"Sky said you're after Mr. Sheridan to be my daddy. I told him that wasn't true and to shut his face." Violet's gaze met Adriana's in the mirror. "Right?"

Adriana's gut clenched. "You should never tell someone to shut their face. That's not polite."

Violet scowled. "But he was lying. You told me never to lie."

Sam closed the book and laid it across his lap. "Some kids told me that, too."

Oh, no. "Who was that?"

Her son shrugged. "A few kids. I don't want to tattle."

Lord, help me out here? I don't know how to assure my children without lying. "Would you two like a dad again someday?"

Violet crossed her arms and narrowed her eyes. "We had a daddy, and he died."

"Well, if Mommy fell in love with… with a man, and married him, he'd live in our house and be your dad. Would you like that?"

Sam pushed his glasses up. "That would be a stepdad, right?"

"Yes. That's what I meant."

"Orson has a stepdad. He doesn't really like him."

"Orson's parents are divorced. That makes it harder for kids when their parents get married again. And it's different from what would happen at our house. I mean, if anything *did* happen, ever."

The kids exchanged a look. "I don't know, Mom." Sam pulled his eyebrows together thoughtfully. "It might be cool to have a dad to do guy things with. Like play catch, maybe. Or go on bike rides."

Not that Adriana hadn't ever done those things with Sam. She even took him to baseball games sometimes. Hockey games. Even an occasional basketball game. But she didn't really enjoy it, other than spending time nurturing her son.

"Mr. Sheridan is pretty nice," Violet told Sam. "I don't think he already has kids. Is he 'vorced?"

Sam scowled. "Dunno. But Orson's stepdad has bigger kids and they're mean."

Time for an intervention. "Mr. Sheridan isn't divorced and he doesn't have any children of his own."

Both kids turned to look at her.

Uh. What had she done? But it did beg the question of whether Myles would feel gypped not having more children. Adriana was already thirty-four. Not too old to carry a pregnancy to term, but not something she'd want to put off several years if Myles wanted babies.

Why again were they putting their relationship on hold

for another five months? Right, for the sake of the little people in the backseat. For the sake of Myles's job. This was crazy. "Hey, have you kids ever wanted to be homeschooled? You know, like the Trenton kids at church. Their mom teaches them their subjects at home."

Sam adjusted his glasses as he frowned at her. "Homeschool? When would I see Caden and Orson? I like Ms. Bertoli. She does fun things with our class, and we have math teams."

"No way," put in Violet. "I like playing with Sabrina and Desiree at recess, and Mr. Sheridan has cool art supplies."

"Besides, you work all the time," said Sam.

"If we did that, I'd spend less time working and more time with you two. We could do fun art projects, too." Not sure how she could manage math teams. "Maybe you'd like to learn to sew, Violet."

The distrust on both faces stared at her in the mirror. For just a few seconds, Adriana had warmed up to the idea herself but, like she'd told her sister, it wasn't a good solution for their family. Guilt poked. Was she shortchanging Myles by not giving it an honest try? Wouldn't it be worth it if they could date openly?

But it wasn't fair to use Violet as a pawn. Adults understood waiting — understood it far too well, anymore. She and Myles had survived almost two months now, but all of winter and most of spring still loomed.

Too long. She couldn't do this. She needed Myles. Needed him in her life every day. Needed his kisses, needed to sleep spooned against his warmth, needing him breezing into the house every day after school and dropping his briefcase in the hall closet before kissing her.

He had become as vital as air.

Something had to give. Had to.

Adriana looked back in the mirror. Sam had opened the dinosaur book again. Violet's headphones cradled her head as she listened to an audio story with her eyes closed.

Maybe that homeschooling thing was their only option. How could she possibly sell Violet on it if she didn't really want to do it herself? Why should Violet make the sacrifice for the adults in her life?

The circles never ended.

"Sweetheart, I don't want to hide anymore. I think it's time we told Violet and Sam." Myles had never felt more daring in his life. Although, real heroes' hands didn't likely sweat until they fumbled their cell phones.

"I'm not sure, Myles. What if it doesn't turn out well? Then we're kind of stuck."

He hated the distance between them. She was way off in Arcadia Valley in southern Idaho, while he paced his dad's living room in Moscow. He stopped and looked out at the houses below, where Christmas trees twinkled through windows. He ached to hold her, kiss her, make her promises for the future, not skulk for months more until the end of the school year.

"It will be fine." Wouldn't it? "Violet likes me. I think she'll be okay with us."

"But Randi said—"

"I know." He hesitated. "Do you think they can keep a secret?"

"For five months?" Adriana's voice sounded incredulous. "I don't think Violet can keep a secret for five minutes. Whatever she's thinking comes straight out her mouth."

That was the ring of truth, right there. And what Violet didn't say, her posture and facial expressions gave away.

"Sam's not very good at secrets, either. Once the cat's out of the bag, there will be no stuffing it back in."

"Won't it be worth it?" They should have had this discussion in person. Frustration ground through Myles. They never had the chance. Ever. It had to end.

"You'll be the one facing Randi. You'll be the one facing Violet every day at school. You know what she's like if things aren't going her way."

At first, Myles had thought Adriana was simply too lax with her daughter, but he'd been proved wrong. She stood as firm as any parent could in the face of such an obstinate child. He'd developed a ruse or two of his own to deal with Violet. Maybe they'd work in this situation, too.

"Adriana, I love you." The words may have come out with a tinge of desperation, but he couldn't take that back. Besides, they were true, desperation and all. "I need you. I need to come by your house in broad daylight. I need to take the kids swimming at the pool and go to their jiu jitsu meets. I need to take you for dinner, to walk along the river holding your hand. I need you."

"I need you, too." Her voice was soft. Full of yearning.

His heart leaped. "I've already reserved a room at the Fairview B&B over New Year's." It wasn't too far from her parents' house where she and the kids were staying. Adriana had said her sister would spend time with the kids so she could get away to be with him. More hiding. "But I want to come openly. Please."

Myles remembered his dad's advice from earlier in the evening, when they'd first returned from the candlelight service at church. How Dad said Myles needed to own up like a man, and not let Adriana call the shots. So far he'd deferred because, after all, Violet and Sam were her kids, not his.

A man wearing a Santa suit wandered down the street below, jingling a set of bells. Myles was missing out on everything about Christmas with the family he hoped would soon be his. Dad was right. A man needed to buck up. He straightened his back. "I'm driving in on the thirtieth. I can get an early start, and the forecast looks clear, so I could be there for lunch. Where can we meet?"

"Are you really sure, Myles?"

He poured certainty into his voice. "Never been surer about anything. Other than that I love you."

"The kids have been asking to go for lunch to The Jukebox, a favorite hangout from when I was a teen. It has that fifties vibe, and it fascinates them both."

"Meet you there at one on the thirtieth?" If he could survive almost a week before driving down. Maybe he should go earlier. Give Violet longer to get used to the situation before school resumed a few days into January. But no, the bed and breakfast was closed over Christmas, or booked. He couldn't remember which. Either way, the dates had been chosen.

"Okay. Should I… prepare them?"

Good question. Myles stared out the window. Santa was long gone. Wait. It was up to Myles to unite them as a family. His heart stilled. Was he really thinking that far in advance? To marry Adriana and embrace her children as his own? Yes, he was. Otherwise this was definitely not worth the gamble.

"I think… I believe it's better if I handle it. But, definitely, let's pray about it together. I want the Lord's will. His blessing."

"Me, too." Her voice echoed the longing he felt.

Myles watched festive lights race along the eaves of the house across the street. "I don't ever want to be apart at Christmas again."

"I love you, Myles."

"I love you, sweetheart. Merry Christmas."

Chapter 17

ADRIANA SAT ACROSS from her children in The Jukebox in Arcadia Valley, watching the door. Her mind battled between the thrill of seeing Myles again — and having their romance out in the open — and dread at putting the situation on the line with Violet and Sam.

Her heart, though, knew what it wanted. It surged as she caught sight of Myles through the large plate glass window as he reached for the restaurant's door handle.

He'd come.

Here we go, Lord. I'm still not sure this is the right thing.

Right or wrong, they were committed now. He glanced around the café and caught sight of her. He stopped for an instant, and she filled her vision with his beloved face as his eyes caressed her, a slow smile spreading across his face.

Adriana bit her lip and returned the smile.

"Mom?" Sam brought her back to the red padded booth with its gray laminate table, unchanged from her teenage years.

"Yes?" Her own voice sound like it reverberated in an echo chamber.

He pushed his glasses up his nose. "I said, can we go to the aquatic center today?"

"Maybe." That might not be a bad idea of something to do with Myles while he was here. He said he loved to swim.

Myles rested his hand on the back of the booth beside Violet's head. "Hi there. Fancy meeting you in Arcadia Valley."

"Myles." Adriana's breath caught. No, she should have called him Mr. Sheridan. The children didn't know they'd leaped that barrier months ago.

Both kids looked up, and a scowl settled on Violet's face. "What are you doing here?" She crossed her arms over her chest and glowered up at him.

This could be going better.

Sam looked between them, his brown eyebrows rising above his glasses' frames.

"Mind if I join you?" asked Myles.

"Please do." Adriana scooted down the padded bench as he slid in beside her. Should she make some small talk? Say what a surprise this was? But that was lying. Putting off the inevitable. No, they'd decided on the phone Christmas Eve that it was time, even if they didn't know how it would work out. They'd played it safe long enough.

Adriana felt like she stood on the top of an unfamiliar cliff in the mist. A voice she trusted — was it God's, Myles's, or both? — told her to leap into the unknown. That it was safe below.

It didn't feel safe.

She reached for Myles's hand, wishing she didn't need to keep any distance between them, that he could wrap his arms around her and kiss her. They'd get to it. Later. So much depended on the next few minutes. Myles's warm fingers clasped hers under the table, out of the children's view.

Sam cleared his throat. "It's a surprise to see you here, Mr. Sheridan."

They'd agreed Myles would take the lead. Adriana hung onto his hand and prayed for dear life.

Myles's fingers tightened on hers. "I wanted to see you guys. Talk to you and Violet."

"Oh? What about?" Sam looked so grownup as he glanced between them.

Violet slouched further against the bench, her scowl etching itself deeper on her face.

"I'm not sure if you two have noticed, but your mom and I have become good friends since I started teaching at Bridgeview Elementary. I like her quite a lot."

Sam's eyes narrowed. "I see." After a few seconds he added, "no, I don't. What do you mean?"

Here went nothing. Adriana reached her free hand across the table to cover Sam's. "What Mr. Sheridan means is that we've been spending time together when we could, getting to know each other. We thought you should know that we are falling in love with each other."

Violet surged to her feet at the end of the table. "How come Sky Romero knew and I didn't? That's not fair, Mom. I don't like you."

"Sky doesn't really know anything." Adriana's arms ached to gather her stubborn daughter close. "His mom was only guessing." And stirring up her kids. "I'm sorry you feel this way. I didn't want to say anything to you until I knew for sure."

Myles nodded, his gaze fixed on Violet. "That's right. It

takes a long time for grownups to know if they're really in love. It's a big decision, and we didn't think it was a good idea for you two to be in the middle of it."

Hands on her hips, Violet glared at Myles. "I already have a daddy. Just because he's in heaven doesn't mean I don't have a dad. I don't need another one."

Sam's gaze flicked between all of them. "I don't know, Violet. It might be nice to have one for real, too. That wouldn't mean our daddy wouldn't still be our dad. Would it, Mom?"

This eight-year-old's wisdom never ceased to amaze her. "You're right, Sam. Stephan Diaz will always be your daddy. He's the one who helped you be born, and no one else can ever do that."

Sam nudged his glasses. "I've been meaning to ask you about tha—"

"Not right now, Sam. Later."

Myles's hand convulsed around Adriana's as a flush crept up her face. Talk about timing. "But you're also right that having a dad living at our house would be fun for you and Violet. He'd be able to do stuff with you that I can't. It's more than that, though."

So, so awkward. She and Myles hadn't pledged unending love to each other. They'd both hinted where they hoped this relationship would go, but he hadn't actually proposed.

"What your mom means is that we love each other. I wouldn't get to be your father without loving your mom and being married to her. We just want to know if you two might be okay with that happening sometime. What do you think?"

No, Myles, no. They'd talked about how to word it, and letting the children think they had control had *not* been on the agenda.

"You're my teacher, not my dad." Violet's eyes spat daggers. "It's not fair."

"Violet, please sit down." How Adriana wished she'd risen when Myles arrived and let him slide into the booth ahead of her. Then she'd be much closer to her daughter. Could reach out and touch her. Gather her in a hug. Not that her obstinate child would likely let her.

"No." Violet stomped her foot. "I don't want you."

"Violet Louise. That's enough. Sit down and stop making a scene. Mr. Sheridan wasn't asking you for permission. He was telling you about something that is already happening."

"I think it might be okay." Sam assessed Myles. "Do you know jiu jitsu?"

Myles parked behind Adriana's car at the curb beside her parents' home. It had taken Adriana half an hour to calm Violet down at the café, and things hadn't gone any better at the aquatic center. He and Sam had spent an hour cannonballing off the diving board, while Violet played with an inflatable raft in the shallow end. Of course, her mother had to stay nearby. The girl was only seven. He could certainly think of more fun ways to spend time with Adriana. He'd barely gotten more than a glimpse of her in that one-piece. Then they'd had supper at a Mexican restaurant owned by a distant relative of Adriana's. What now?

Lord, what do we do here? We've fallen in love and believed we had Your blessing. But Violet—

He groaned and rubbed his hands over his face. Would Adriana's parents and sister have any better a reaction to him than Violet? Man, he'd known she was a stubborn one. He hadn't been her teacher for four months without figuring that out.

Sam stood at Myles's car window with his eyebrows raised. Adriana waited at the end of the sidewalk. Violet was nowhere in sight.

Myles rubbed the boy's shoulder and took Adriana's hand. See, they could be a family, if Violet was only willing to give him a chance.

"I'm sorry about Violet," began Adriana, not for the first time.

"It's okay." Myles squeezed her fingers. But it wasn't. Not really. "We'll figure it out."

The front door opened, and a trim middle-aged man stood in the opening wearing gray dress pants and a white shirt, open at the collar.

"Dad, I'd like you to meet Myles Sheridan. Myles, this is my dad, Duane."

The man's face was expressionless. Myles let go of Adriana's hand to shake her father's. "Pleased to meet you."

Duane Silva had a strong grip and a penetrating gaze. "I'd like to say the same, but my granddaughter ran inside yelling that she hates you both."

"Violet's being silly," Sam announced, looking between the adults.

Myles cleared his throat. "I, uh, I don't know what to say. Until a few hours ago, I was pretty sure she liked me."

Adriana let out a long breath. "Scoot along inside and play with your sister, Sam."

He scowled at his mother. "But—"

"Sam."

"Fine." Sam edged past his grandfather and kicked off

his snow boots.

"Can we come in now, Dad? You're paying to heat the entire street. Possibly we are also providing entertainment."

Duane stepped aside. Deep inside the house, a door slammed. Adriana unzipped her tall boots, a worried frown on her face, and her dad took her coat before Myles could reach for it.

"I should go talk to Violet."

Her father shook his head. "Alaina's got her for now. Let her handle it."

This was not how Myles had envisioned meeting Adriana's family. His gut twisted at the memory of the little girl's fury. Adriana would be torn, and it looked like her dad was on Violet's side. Was there any other side to take?

It was going to get a thousand times worse when they were all back in Bridgeview, and school resumed next week. Randi Philson had been oh, so right.

Myles followed Adriana up the half-flight to the living room of the bi-level house. She took a seat in a wing-back chair. It had already begun. How could he gain any comfort or confidence in the way things were progressing if he couldn't sit next to her and feel her touch? He sat on the nearest end of a deep floral sofa while her dad settled into a leather recliner.

"Where's Mom? I should help with dinner." Adriana started to rise.

Her dad waved her back to her seat. "Your mother's fine. What I want to know is, what you two are going to do about this."

Adriana sent Myles a furtive glance. "I'm not sure, Daddy. I wasn't expecting this reaction from Violet. For months she's told me how much she likes Myles."

"As a teacher." Duane's eyebrows rose.

"Well, yes, of course. But it didn't seem a big jump to think she liked him as a person and could accept him into the rest of her life."

"I don't know what you were thinking, Adriana."

Heat began to rise under Myles's collar. How dare her father talk to her that way? Adriana was thirty-four years old. An adult. She'd been a wife and was still a mother, and a darn good one considering the volatile child. No wonder she lived in Spokane, far from her family.

"With all due respect, Mr. Silva, it's not like we planned to fall in love." Myles leaned forward, his elbows on his knees. "Neither of us were looking for a relationship, yet we believe God brought us together."

"You understand it's hard for me to see that perspective when it makes my only granddaughter so upset. I'd think, if God were for it, He'd smooth the way a bit better than He's done."

"Daddy, you know that's not true."

Duane's gaze swung to his daughter. "Pardon me?"

"That's not how God works. He's not a... a Good Housekeeping Seal of Approval." Adriana fidgeted with the hem of her burgundy sweater. "When things are easy, it doesn't mean it's God's will any more than if things are hard, it isn't. Otherwise no true believers would ever suffer hardship of any kind."

"So you're going to carry on against your daughter's wishes?"

Myles blinked. His collar tightened around his throat. Indeed, his shirt squeezed his entire torso, and the air in the room seemed too thin to breathe. How could this be happening?

"You're putting words in my mouth, Daddy."

She wouldn't send Myles away, would she? They could work this out... but better at home in Bridgeview than here with her father's negative presence.

"I just want what's best for you, princess. You and the children. I know you've had it tough since Stephan died, but that doesn't mean you need to take the first—"

"Dad, that's enough. If all I'd wanted was to find some other man, I wouldn't have waited five years."

"If you moved back home, we could help out more. Violet is a challenge, and she needs a strong influence." Duane glanced at Myles then back to Adriana. "You and the children could live in the basement here. I think that would be the best solution."

Adriana surged to her feet. "I disagree. Yes, she's a handful, but I'm not tearing her away from the only home she's ever known. We live in Spokane, Dad. *That's* our home. Our life."

Myles silently cheered her on as the bands constricting his breathing loosened slightly.

"You're making a big mistake, princess," Duane said quietly.

"Just like when I went to college in Spokane? Just like when I married Stephan? Just like when we didn't wait ten years to get pregnant?" She crossed her arms over her chest. "Myles isn't a mistake. Any more than Gonzaga U was. Than Stephan or the children were. I thought you were done trying to run my life, but if you're starting back up again, the kids and I will be driving back to Spokane tomorrow. I don't need this."

Myles gripped his sweating hands together. Should he get up and stand beside Adriana in a show of support? Stay where he was and be glad she didn't let her father dictate her life? Man, he hated confrontation. Always had, and it wasn't any more fun being the reason for it than one of the contestants.

Stand.

He rose and took the few steps to Adriana, reaching for her hand. When her arms remained clenched around herself, he slid his around her waist and turned to Duane. "I love your daughter, Mr. Silva. I hope you'll come to accept that we're adults who will make the best decisions we can — not only for ourselves, but for Violet and Sam."

Was it his imagination, or did Adriana lean slightly against him now? He rubbed his hand along the curve of her hip, refusing to still it even when Duane's gaze lingered there.

"Sis?" A female voice came from behind them.

Adriana turned. "Hey, Alaina. I'd like you to meet Myles. Myles, this is my sister, Alaina."

Alaina looked like a younger version of Adriana, nearly as pretty. She flashed a smile at him. "Nice to meet you, Myles. Ads, I thought you'd want to know that Violet is ready for bed. I think she's running a bit of a fever."

Adriana pulled away from Myles. "I'll come tuck her in."

Her children would always come first. Wasn't that how it should be? But did that leave only a sliver of space in her life for Myles? Was that enough? The raised eyebrows of her father challenged the thought.

Chapter 18

AFTER ONE LAST HICCUP, Violet's tear-stained face finally relaxed into slumber. Adriana smoothed the damp hair away from her daughter's forehead. This had been the closest thing to a tantrum Violet had indulged in for months. Who knew the thought of her mom falling in love with her teacher would set her off like this?

Myles had been alone with her parents and sister for over an hour while Adriana settled Violet. Or maybe he'd given up and headed over to Fairview Bed & Breakfast, where he'd booked a room. Adriana couldn't blame him if he had. Although, if she were the abandoned one, she'd probably be westbound on I-84 by now, determined to put this melodramatic family behind her. She'd be thankful for a lucky escape.

Adriana rose and tucked the blanket around Violet's chest before crossing to look at her son. Sam lay sprawled on the twin bed across the room, his breath even. How he'd fallen asleep with all that racket was beyond comprehension. She pressed a kiss to his brow and slipped into the corridor as quietly as she could.

Alaina's laugh broke the silence as Adriana came around the corner. Myles bent over a game of checkers from his spot on the sofa, while Alaina sat cross-legged on a cushion across the coffee table. Both looked up.

"She's asleep." Probably one of the dumbest announcements she'd ever made. "Who's winning?"

"Me, of course," announced Alaina smugly, zigzagging a checker across the board.

Adriana's gaze tried to catch Myles's, but he stared down at the game. She sat next to him on the sofa, shoulder and leg pressed against his. "Where are Mom and Dad?"

Alaina rolled her eyes. "I sent them to fix coffee and dessert so Dad would stop glowering at Myles."

"That bad?" Adriana nudged Myles.

He glanced over with a quick lopsided grin. "Pretty much."

"Oh, no."

"They'll come around, Ads. You know they only want what's best for you."

"And they're taking their cue from Violet. Because a seven-year-old should have veto power."

Alaina tucked a long strand of hair behind her ear. "I'll agree your kid has set the tone as far as her grandparents are concerned. It caught them off guard is all."

Her parents weren't the only ones caught off guard. "They could have trusted me instead of falling for Violet's outburst. They didn't even give Myles a chance."

"I know Mom was hurt you hadn't told her he was coming until yesterday. They didn't have a chance to warm up to the idea before your kid had a hissy fit. No one wants to hear a child spew 'I hate you' at her mother."

"No mother wants to hear it," Adriana said softly. She

should have stopped in the bathroom and found some painkillers for the headache that was now in full bloom.

"Look, I'm sorry. It seems to be my fault." Myles leaned on the sofa arm away from Adriana. He still wasn't fully meeting her gaze. "I thought she was ready to hear about us, but I was mistaken. I handled this all wrong."

"There might never have been a better time until she turned twenty."

"The better time would have been after the school year ended. I just... just didn't want to keep living like this, hiding our relationship as though we were teens sneaking around after curfew."

She rubbed his thigh. Why didn't he stretch his hand to cover hers? "I know. I hated that part too."

"Now what?" Alaina looked from one to the other.

Myles shook his head. "I was planning to stay a couple of days, but I'm not sure that's a good idea. I don't want to cause any more issues and ruin the rest of your family's Christmas break."

Adriana wanted to assure him that he hadn't, but it wasn't completely true. Everything had been going pretty well until noon today. It wasn't Myles's fault, exactly. It was hers just as much for not finding a way to ease the kids into the idea. For not opening up to her parents. They'd messed up, and the consequences stared them in the face. "Please don't leave early. We haven't even had a chance to spend any time together, just us."

"I volunteer to put the kids to bed tomorrow so you two can go out for New Year's Eve. El Corazon has an evening buffet and live salsa music. Dancing."

Myles bit his lip.

If he didn't stay, Adriana was going to lose him for good.

163

How she knew, she couldn't have said. Maybe she was going to anyway, but not without a fight. "Or we could do something else. Bigby Farm might have a hay ride scheduled. Or we could go over to your B&B and talk." By talk, she meant kiss.

"Not the B&B. They're having a bunch of people over for a party." He sent her a pleading look. "I just don't know what to do."

She tugged his hand over and laced her fingers through his. "Please, Myles. Don't give up so easily. You're here. Let's see how we can salvage the visit."

He clung to her as though she were a lifeline. "Are you sure?"

Alaina rose. "I'll keep our parents in the kitchen a bit longer." She tossed a wink over her shoulder as she left the room.

"I'm very sure." Adriana twisted on the sofa, wrapped her arms around his neck, and pressed her lips to his. "Please," she whispered.

Myles's arms slipped around her as he kissed her. "I don't remember how to live without you anymore."

"There's no need to remember," she murmured.

Myles jogged along the Canyon Walk in nearby Twin Falls. It was going to be a very long day until he could spend time alone with Adriana. It was only mid-morning, but she'd already canceled lunch with him, citing Violet. He had no doubt the reason was accurate. The big question was, could he live his entire life on the sidelines of Adriana's love and attention? He knew she loved him.

It was Violet.

And then there were the comments Duane had made last night when Adriana was out of the room. He'd made sure Myles knew what a great man Stephan had been. Bigger than life. A hero in every way.

So not like Myles. He didn't have the other man's charismatic personality. His bravery. He was himself: rather unsure, rather held back. He'd felt so daring pursuing Adriana in secret. Stephan would never have done that. The man had been all 'go big or go home.'

Myles was in over his head. He wasn't that guy. How could he compete with Adriana's memories? Her dad clearly thought he couldn't.

And Duane wasn't the worst of it. Last night, neither of them had mentioned the elephant in the room. What was going to happen when school resumed next Tuesday? He'd gambled on winning Violet over — such an unusual act of bravery — and lost. How would she react to him in class? How would he be able to treat her as he had before? He should have listened to Randi. She'd spoken wisdom.

Maybe he should resign. There were substitute teachers to fill in. He could move away — Florida might be far enough — and pick up some sub jobs until he could find something permanent again. Or try his hand at construction work. Something. Anything that got him out of Violet Diaz's range.

Myles dodged an elderly couple walking their Chihuahua and continued pounding down the concrete walkway, breathing the crisp winter air. The Snake River wound its way between deep canyon walls lined with volcanic rock, partially hidden by rising mist. An epic flood like that of Noah's day would be required to make the river rise the nearly five hundred feet to give the water an option besides the northwest direction the canyon channeled the flow. He felt just as hemmed in as the river, carried along by the current of events that had begun the day he'd realized he was falling in love with Adriana Diaz.

He should have bailed out of that boat the first moment he'd known he was in it. He should have guessed that nothing good could come of it... but it was hard to regret the stolen kisses they'd shared.

Oh, Adriana.

Panting heavily, he veered into a viewpoint with its curving wrought-iron railing. Fog blanketed the view. He hated the obscurity. He needed to clearly see into the distance, see what he was up against.

What was it Adriana had said? *Faith is the substance of things hoped for, the evidence of things not seen.* The mist didn't matter. It didn't change reality, just the perception of it.

Reality was that Violet was completely against their relationship. She had more than ten years left before leaving home. Sure, she might change her mind eventually, but did Myles want to wait until he was over forty to claim the woman he loved?

Maybe instead of thinking about faith, he should remember the saying about God closing a door but opening a window. Maybe Adriana wasn't the woman for him. Maybe he'd meet someone else. Someone who wasn't as outgoing and demanding as Adriana, or even Dakota. Someone who didn't have children at all, let alone in the class he was teaching. Someone with whom he could build a quiet, peaceful life. No drama.

But... Adriana. How could he let her go?

She's asleep.

Adriana glanced at the text, and a wave of relief washed over her. She'd felt so much guilt leaving the children with her sister when everything set Violet off again.

"Things okay?" asked Myles.

She tipped her phone toward him. "Sounds like it is, now. Want to go back to the house? Alaina will stay upstairs, and my parents will be at the church until after midnight." Grace Fellowship partied hearty with board games and snacks throughout the evening and then a watchnight prayer service. Some New Year's Eves Adriana had enjoyed attending. It held no attraction this year. Not compared to finally having some time with Myles where they weren't making out in the backseat of his car like a pair of hormone-driven teens.

"Will Violet *stay* asleep?"

Adriana couldn't fault him for wondering. "She usually does. My sister will listen for her and Sam."

Myles nodded and opened the car door. Soon they were rearranged in the front, the car in gear. He'd been so quiet this evening, his kisses bordering on desperation. Not that he'd pushed the limits with his hands. If anything, he'd been more careful than ever. What was going on inside his head? He was so hard to read.

Soon they were curled up on the family room sofa downstairs with a movie and a bowl of popcorn. Myles didn't seem to find the comedic bits as funny as she did, and she snuck a glance at him. He stared off, his lower lip caught between his teeth.

"Myles?" She put the movie on pause. "Want to talk about it?"

He blinked and focused on her face. "I'm sorry. I missed that part."

"I think you've missed half the movie."

"Probably." He grimaced. "Sorry to be such bad company."

She kept her voice light. "Next you're going to be sorry for saying sorry so many times."

"I probably should be."

"Myles, I love you. That hasn't changed just because my daughter is capable of a hissy fit worthy of any two-year-old on the planet."

His hand caressed her shoulder. "I love you, too."

"I sense the word 'but' in there."

"I don't see how this is going to work," he murmured, blue eyes fixed on hers.

Adriana's gut twisted. "We're adults. We can make it work."

His brows rose slightly. "Like you can bend Violet to your will just like that?"

"She'll come around. I know she will."

"Sweetheart, in five days, school goes back in. I'll stand at the front of my classroom, and she'll take a seat at her table with Desiree and Sabrina. How do you think that day is going to play out?"

"It will be fine—"

"You really think so? You think she'll have forgotten all about this in under a week? That she'll cooperate with me in class? That the other kids won't notice the tension between us? That Sky Romero won't tease her and tell his mother? That Randi Philson won't call me into her office?"

Adriana pressed a finger over his lips. "Where's your faith?"

168

"Where's your grip on reality?"

What? She withdrew her touch. While she was at it, she surged to her feet, breaking all contact. "I can't believe you said that."

"I can't believe you're living in a fairyland where conflict is no bigger than what's for tea."

She straightened and wrapped her arms around herself. "And you're borrowing a heap of trouble that might never happen. I've met trouble, Myles Sheridan. Trouble far more shattering than 'what will people think?'. We've let the cat out of the bag, and there's no stuffing it back in. So, instead of bemoaning the possible trials to come, how about we just brace up and ride the wave? It will work out."

"Bemoaning?"

He would grab that one word out of what she'd said. Although the word described what he was doing perfectly. She softened her voice. "Myles, we have something special. Don't let fear take it away."

"It's my job on the line here. It's—"

"It's something you should have thought of before sneaking into my house that night in October."

"I didn't sneak in. I rang the doorbell. You opened the door."

Adriana clamped her lips tight over the words that wanted to pour out. Did she actually want to drive him away? No. His love had given her a new lease on life. She'd been able to focus on a bright future with the memories tucked away where they belonged. Stephan was her past. Myles was her future.

He stared at her, blue eyes as cold as they'd been that August day when they'd first met.

She shivered. Had she already said too much? "Myles, I

169

love you. Love doesn't keep record of wrongs. It clings to the truth. Please."

"Adriana, I just don't know how to do this. I really don't. Yes, it's possible for time heal it all, but we've only got five days. We need a miracle."

"Then let's pray for one."

"You think I haven't been?"

Of course, he had. Probably more than she'd been. "Together. United." She stood in front of him, stretching both hands toward him.

He didn't take them.

A thought jumped into her mind and popped out of her mouth. "We have time to fly to Vegas and back before school starts again."

From the shocked look on his face, yes, she'd really said that out loud. Proposed to elope with him. Well, why not? Although… she knew a thousand reasons why not, and two of them were asleep upstairs. "Okay, maybe not that. Although it's not a horrible idea."

Myles surged to his feet. "Adriana, you'd regret that for the rest of your life. You don't do impulsive any more than I do."

Compared to him, she was a bit of dandelion fluff dancing in a summer wind. "Sure, I do."

"Name something. You're the epitome of a solid person. You've lived in the same house for, what, ten years? Created jobs to work around your children's schedules. Your neighbors know they can count on you."

All true. "But you did something impulsive when you left a secure job to teach at Bridgeview. Why?"

His gaze narrowed. "A woman. A fellow teacher who wouldn't take no for an answer."

Oh, boy. She'd never have guessed that one.

"I'm going back to the B&B now and heading back to Washington first thing in the morning."

"The movie's not over. It's not even midnight." She reached for him, and he caught her hands, preventing her from wrapping her arms around him.

"I love you, Adriana. Happy New Year." He brushed a swift kiss across her lips and was gone.

Chapter 19

MYLES STRODE INTO Bridgeview Elementary half an hour before classes resumed after Christmas break. He hadn't felt less ready to face his students than at his very first school eight years before.

He'd read — over and over — every one of the emails and texts Adriana had sent since New Year's Eve, though he hadn't replied to a single one of them. Today he needed to talk to Randi.

Too late. Adriana sat on the edge of a chair in the school lobby, the principal beside her. The two women were deep in conversation.

Myles's heart stopped beating when Adriana glanced up and saw him standing there. Makeup had done little to camouflage the dark circles under her eyes, and the sparkle he loved so much was completely absent.

He'd done that to her. Drawn her out then shoved her back into the mist by his insistence on coming to Arcadia Valley over vacation. By being in her life at all. He'd toyed with her, played her like a violin — no, that was ridiculous. He'd fallen in love. So had she. But it was not to be. Not now.

Probably not ever.

Randi turned and caught his eye over her shoulder. "Mr. Sheridan, please join us for a moment."

"Certainly, Ms. Philson. I hope you had a good vacation." He pulled a chair around and straddled it, careful not to look at Adriana.

"Very nice, thank you. But Ms. Diaz has brought something to my attention that is more than a little troubling."

The principal thought *she* was troubled? Try living his life. But... it did affect her. Affect the school. His job.

"I'm sorry." He'd never been more sorry about anything in his entire life. Myles pulled the folded paper from his chest pocket and handed it to Randi. "Maybe this will help."

Her eyes tracked back and forth across the few lines then she refolded the paper. "No, this does not help." She held it back toward him.

"Myl..." Adriana's voice cracked. "Mr. Sheridan, I'm going to be homeschooling Violet. I've come for her things."

"No, that's not the solution." Myles pushed the paper back at Randi. "This is."

"What's in there?"

Without a word, Randi handed the letter to Adriana, who read it, head shaking. "No. Myles. You can't do this."

Randi's arms crossed as she looked from one to the other. "Exactly what *did* happen over the past two weeks? Last I knew, a couple of months ago, you'd both agreed to wait until after the school year was over. I take it that didn't happen."

It was all his fault. He was the one who'd knocked on Adriana's door that night. The one who'd insisted the kids were ready.

"Not exactly," murmured Adriana. "We were very circumspect, getting to know each other through emails. No

173

one knew save a few very close friends."

Randi nodded, eyebrows raised.

"We met a couple of times, far away from Spokane. W-we fell in love."

Myles's heart broke all over again. "It was my fault. I thought it was time the children knew. I came to Adriana's parents' place last week." He paused. "Violet reacted badly."

"Very badly," whispered Adriana.

The principal's gaze shuttered as she shook her head. "There are so many things I could say right now, starting with 'I told you so' and going on from there. You've put the school in an extremely awkward position."

"That's why I'm resigning." Myles stared at his shoe. "I'm the one who should have known better. I did know better, but I let my emotions carry me away."

"Myles, you can't resign." Adriana's hand touched his arm then withdrew. "It's not all your fault. I'm just as much to blame. I welcomed you."

"One moment." Randi rose. "I'll send Diana to your classroom, Myles. The bell is about to ring."

The school receptionist? He stumbled to his feet. "If you'll accept my resignation, I'll go myself."

"Not so quickly, Mr. Sheridan." The principal's gaze quelled his thoughts and pushed him back into the chair. "I'll be right back." She crossed the lobby amid the stream of chattering students.

Adriana stood. "I'll get my daughter's things from the classroom and be on my way. Rebekah has an appointment in an hour, so she can't watch Violet for long."

"No," he protested. "You can't teach her at home. If any child needs a school environment, it's Violet."

"There aren't any other options." Adriana's voice held an

edge. "It's just until the end of the term."

"Are you a trained teacher? No, you're not. Violet has special needs—"

"She tests perfectly normally."

He pushed on. "She'll be behind her classmates when she comes back in fall. She needs socialization with her peers. There are all kinds of reasons this is a horrible idea."

"We both know there's no alternative." An edge came to Adriana's voice, reminding him of the woman he'd first met in August. "If you'd answered my emails, we could have at least discussed things, but no, you cut me off." She leaned closer. "That's not how love works, Myles Sheridan. Love puts up with anything and everything that comes along. It trusts, hopes, and endures no matter what. Check it out. First Corinthians thirteen."

He sucked in a deep breath. "Sometimes love isn't the right way forward. Sometimes it's too messy."

"You're telling me you're planning to resign, move away from Bridgeview, and cut me out of your life, all in one fell swoop? That *that* is a better option?"

Her direct words forced a nod out of him. The little kid in him cringed. Hid.

"You know what, Myles? Life *is* messy. Love is messy. We're all just human beings trying to get through the best way we can, and we fail, often. But God is faithful, if we just keep throwing ourselves at His feet. He will show a path, and I'm pretty sure it's not you running away."

"Running away?" He straightened. Looked up. Nearly dissolved in her fiery gaze.

"What would you call it?"

"Stepping aside. Allowing your life to resume. Making it easier for Violet."

"How about fighting for what you want? How about growing a backbone?"

He surged to his feet. "There's a time for fighting, and there's a time for admitting you made a mistake. Stepping back."

"Now I'm a mistake?" She leaned in, her nose inches from his. "If that's how you really feel, then I guess I am."

She was so close he could feel the heat of her body. Smell her minty breath. He wanted to kiss her with every fiber of his being. Tell her he was wrong. That Vegas was a great destination, and let the chips fall where they may. She was worth it.

Myles took a step back, ramming his calf against the chair. Adriana was worth it, but then there was Violet. Violet who had screamed words of hate at him just a few days ago. "You're not a mistake, Adriana, but loving you... is. When I'm gone, your life will be back to normal."

Adriana spat out her words. "Normal is over-rated. I don't want to go back to that place, Myles. I don't want to live in the fog."

He tried again. "Violet will love school again. Sam will—" What about the little boy? He'd assessed Myles from behind those dark-rimmed glasses and decided he was okay.

"Sam will be heartbroken. He already is."

Myles shoved his hands through his hair. "What do you want me to do?"

She crossed her arms over her chest. "Figure it out, Myles."

"So you want me to get fired instead of resigning."

Her eyebrows rose.

"There aren't a whole lot of choices here."

"I'm homeschooling Violet for the rest of second grade.

That opens up every needed option."

"No. She needs the structure of school. She needs a qualified teacher."

"She's seven years old, Myles. We're not talking about how she'll score on her SAT exams."

His head would not stop shaking. "No, Violet is innocent. She shouldn't be a pawn in this game. I can't imagine her approving."

"She's angry."

The tiny hope shriveled.

"You know what, Myles? It isn't all about how Violet feels about you or school. Yes, in your classroom it's kind of important. But outside of it, she is not queen of the universe. I've let her have too much leeway, but Rebekah is going to help me work with her. She has a psych degree, you know. She counseled here at BES before Olivia was born. We are going to get through this."

From behind him, Randi cleared her throat. "I was going to suggest counseling for Violet. She's quite a strong-willed, demanding child."

Adriana bit her lip. "I know."

"As for you, Mr. Sheridan, I am not accepting this letter. You're a valuable asset to Bridgeview Elementary, and I don't want to lose you over this temporary problem."

Temporary? It was his entire life she was messing with.

"Ms. Diaz, I'll accompany you to the classroom for Violet's things. When we return, Mr. Sheridan, you may go in and send Diana back to the office. We will not be making any other hasty decisions without due process."

Feeling like that long ago child in the principal's presence, Myles nodded. "Yes, ma'am."

177

"I don't want to be homeschooled!" yelled Violet.

Thankfully, Adriana had waited until she and her daughter were back in their own house before dropping the bombshell.

"You also don't want to be in Mr. Sheridan's classroom." Violet had made that clear enough.

"I want to be with Desiree and Sabrina. I don't want to be home all by myself."

Adriana forced out a smile. "You won't be alone. I'll be here with you."

Violet scowled.

"Do you want to talk about why you don't like Mr. Sheridan?"

The little girl's legs swung furiously from her seat on a kitchen stool. "He's mean."

"When someone is mean, it's because they said nasty things to you or tried to hurt you. Did Mr. Sheridan do that?"

She shook her head.

"Then what did he do that's mean?"

"You know." Violet's voice was quieter now.

"Are you angry because he likes Mommy?" If that were even true anymore. No, Adriana had to believe it was. She and Violet might be more trouble than they were worth, especially considering the current nightmare, but Myles's love couldn't be turned off like a light switch. Could it? She remembered the flat look in his eyes earlier at the school, and her heart sank. Maybe it could.

"I want my daddy back."

"Sweetheart, Daddy is in heaven. People can't come back from heaven."

"Why? I need him. Not just any old daddy. My own." Her lower lip quivered.

How Adriana had begged God for the same thing. "When people die, they can't come back and be alive again. That person is gone, and the ones who are left have to accept it."

"But it's not fair."

"Sweetie, lots of things in life aren't fair. Do you think it's fair to Sky that his parents got a divorce and now he hardly ever gets to see his dad?"

"But his daddy's not in heaven. He's in Kennewick."

"That's true, but he also doesn't live at their house anymore. Sky's brother and sister miss their dad, too." Why was she trying to make it be the same thing? It wasn't. She knew it. Violet knew it. "Lots of kids have problems. Lots of other kids have only a mom or only a dad. Some kids don't have enough food or a comfy bed to sleep in."

Violet glared at her.

Okay, so her daughter wasn't ready for empathy. Wasn't ready to hear about orphans in third world countries. Although — guilt chewed at Adriana — she should look into sponsoring a child through an aid agency. Maybe let Violet and Sam each pick one. Would that help?

Today's problem, though, was Violet's anger toward Myles. Even if the situation had escalated so much that Myles would never speak to her again, Adriana couldn't let this go. But… they'd get over this hump, wouldn't they? Her heart had been reawakened to love, but she couldn't simply thank Myles for that and move on. No, it was the man himself who had captured her heart.

She couldn't live without him.

But would living *with* him be an option?

"Violet, I want you to know I will always love Daddy. He was a very special man, and he loved us very much. He loved me, and he loved you and Sam. He was a good father who changed your diapers and cuddled you and sang songs to you. He carried you in a baby carrier like Wade carries baby Olivia."

Tears dribbled down Violet's cheeks. "I don't even remember."

"No, you were only two years old when he died. You wouldn't remember. But it's still true." How to transition from here? "You know that God created people, right? It was His plan to make them into families. To make women and men who would love each other and promise to stay married to each other and take care of their babies together."

"But then why did God make Daddy die?"

"He didn't *make* him die, sweetie. Daddy died in a fire. It was his job to rescue people and put out fires." Adriana pushed aside the memory of that horrible night. "Even though I will always love your dad, I want to love somebody again. I want to have a husband who can help me take care of you and Sam. Who can do things with us and make us laugh."

"I don't like Mr. Sheridan. He's my teacher."

"You used to like him. You told me stories about all the fun things you did at school. You liked painting that eggplant."

"I don't like him anymore."

"I'm sorry to hear that. He's still a very nice man." Adriana's heart cracked. "But I don't think it's a good idea for him to be your teacher."

"I want Mrs. Lopez, like Sam."

And then Adriana would never have met Myles. She would never have known love could sweep her away again. "Mrs. Lopez moved far away, sweetie. She can't come back. So, just for a few months, I'll be your teacher at home. We'll have a good time. I'll read lots of stories to you, and teach you your math. We'll do projects together. It will be fun. You'll see."

Violet's lip curled.

"And in August, you can go back to school and be in third grade with Ms. Bertoli."

She and Myles should have waited. *Definitely* should have. It was too late now. Maybe too late for everything.

Chapter 20

MYLES STARED AT THE teaching material spread out on his kitchen table. This was stupid. It was late January, and snow still covered parts of the schoolyard. No seed in its right mind would sprout in that frigid greenhouse. He was tired of talking about apples and squash for an hour every Tuesday afternoon. The students were tired of doing apple crafts.

Once Adriana had guided this segment of class. At first, she'd done it in person and, after his ill-advised visit to her home — oh, those kisses! — she'd done it via email.

Sometime in the past month she'd stopped emailing him. Stopped texting him. Given up on him, probably, which was just as well, since he'd given up on himself.

If only Bianca Lopez had left less material to sift through. Had left a clear, week by week plan. She hadn't. She'd been an enthusiastic collector of everything that had the vaguest relationship with teaching children the fine arts of gardening.

His next school wouldn't have a gardening module. Wouldn't have a volatile second-grader with whose mother he'd fall in love. Nope. He'd guard himself much more closely in the future. Being a bachelor until his death in old age didn't sound so bad.

Who was he kidding? Myles surged to his feet and poured a glass of water just as a knock sounded on the door to his suite. Who? What? He crossed the space and found Francesca, bearing a covered tray, with Tad right behind her in the doorway.

He'd been avoiding them, too. Avoiding everyone.

"Hi. Can we come in?" But Fran didn't wait for a reply. She edged past him and set the tray on the counter. "I brought apple strudel."

Apple again? But the fragrance of cinnamon tickled at his nostrils. "Uh, hi. Come on in."

Tad offered a lopsided grin as he closed the door behind him. "We hadn't seen you in a while, so we decided to drop by."

"I've been busy."

"Too busy for friends?" Fran offered him a plate of strudel. "We're concerned about you. We haven't even seen you at church."

"I've been attending elsewhere." The one Sunday he'd gone, anyway.

Tad settled onto the sofa with Fran and took a bite of the dessert. "Mmm, this is terrific, love."

"Thanks." Fran pointed her fork at Myles. "You haven't tried it yet."

Why was the world full of so many overbearing women? Myles tasted the dessert and managed a smile. "Very good, thanks." He lowered himself into the easy chair across from them.

"So, uh, anything you want to talk about?" asked Tad.

"What, you guys got a babysitter tonight and couldn't think of anywhere else to go?"

Tad dug into his pocket and set his phone on the coffee table. "Baby monitor app. We'll hear if the kids wake up. No problem."

"Adriana told me you'd decided to let the children in on the secret."

Of course she'd told Fran. Weren't they best friends? The two of them and Rebekah Roper and Juanita, the pastor's wife. As outgoing as Adriana was, she was probably best friends with everyone in Bridgeview. "It was a mistake. Everything."

Fran angled her head. "Want to explain why? I mean, I can understand about how telling Violet backfired, but what do you mean by everything?"

Adriana had rocked his world. He'd been swept away, but now his feet were under him again. He didn't like being vulnerable. "I'd rather not talk about it. It's over. I've started looking for a new position for next school year."

"Tieri will be disappointed to hear that. She can't wait to be in your classroom when she's old enough."

Myles shrugged, hardening his heart. "It can't be helped."

"Sure it can. Adriana is homeschooling Violet. Now there isn't a Diaz child in your class. Isn't this the perfect solution? Why aren't you taking her on dates? Moving things ahead?"

"I told you. It was all a mistake. I should never have let things get that far." And now she was homeschooling her daughter. What state-licensed teacher would go along with an inane plan like that? He couldn't.

A full-bodied cry came from Tad's phone, faintly echoed

naturally through the ceiling. Fran snatched up the phone. "That's Luca. I'll go check on them." She gave Tad a meaningful look, and he nodded.

The door clicked shut behind Fran, leaving an awkward silence. Maybe not as awkward as her questions, though. Maybe Myles and Tad could talk football or something. Super Bowl was coming soon. Who had even advanced to the playoffs?

"So… do you love her?"

Myles blinked at Tad. "I thought I did, but what is love, anyway? Seems like all it brings is pain."

Tad met his gaze directly. "It's not something you can just turn off. From what I hear, Adriana is taking it pretty hard."

"I didn't mean to hurt her." Myles set the dessert plate down.

"Isn't she worth fighting for?"

"How do you fight a seven-year-old?"

"She's just a kid, Myles. Kids grow up. Learn things. Change. You're a teacher. You should know that."

He cringed inside. "She's impenetrable."

"Have you even tried? Have you gone over to their house and done things with her and Sam, tried to win her over? Let her see how much you love her mother?"

Myles shook his head. "She'll reject me."

"How are you giving a child so much power over your life, Myles? What are you really afraid of?"

Rejection. His dad rejected the family. His mom rejected her sons. It was so much easier not to let himself be in a situation where someone could harm him that way again. He'd poked his nose out from under his shell, and look where that had gotten him. The pure hatred of a small child. Not only that, but one who'd idolized him only weeks before.

"No." Myles rose. "I'm not having this conversation."

"Listen, man. We're praying for you, Fran and me. But are *you* praying? Are you seeking God, or have you just decided life's too hard?" Tad stood and gave Myles a swift thump on the back before he could shift away. "Don't lean on your own understanding, Myles. In all your ways acknowledge God, and He *will* direct your path."

"He's a stubborn man." Fran twirled her cup of peppermint tea on the table at Adriana's.

Adriana let an unladylike snort escape. Her friends had joined together in ambush. "Tell me something I hadn't already figured out."

"Is he worth it?" Fran wanted to know. "Maybe it's better just to let things go."

A tiny piece of Adriana's heart died. "I don't know. I think he is worth it, but he's built such a solid fortress around himself in the past few weeks, I don't even know what to do anymore."

"Sometimes you have to let people go their own way," Rebekah put in. "And then, sometimes they come back into your life when you least expect it."

Rebekah should know. She'd broken up with Wade and been reunited with him four years later. Four long years.

"I don't have that much time to waste. I'm already thirty-four. I know what I want."

"So did Wade." Rebekah's voice was so quiet Adriana strained to hear. "It was really hard for him to sit back and wait for me to be ready."

186

It did no good to remind her friend that she dreamed of having babies with Myles. One or two before the risks became too great. She'd thought her life was full with Sam and Violet, but that was before Myles entered it. With him closed off, everything was empty. Meaningless, as King Solomon put it in Ecclesiastes.

"Have you done any more thinking about starting that at-home restaurant business we talked about last fall?"

Adriana turned to Fran. "Some. I decided to wait until spring, when there's fresh produce again. To do it the way I dreamed, it would be fairly seasonal. From May or so through October, maybe as late as Thanksgiving." Her zest for the plan had faded away in the past few weeks, along with her enthusiasm for everything else.

"How about hosting a teacher appreciation dinner?" Rebekah leaned in. "My school's PTA in Tacoma did that, and a bunch of the parents provided the meal. The teachers were surprised and thrilled at the extra recognition."

Fran angled her head. "Exactly what are you thinking?"

Rebekah glanced between them. "Well, Adriana wants to have dinners here. Why not start with inviting the teachers and some of the parents? We can help put it together. I bet Randi would be on board with helping us surprise the teachers."

"No." Adriana's head was already shaking. "If you're thinking Myles would come, you're mistaken. He's not speaking to me at all."

"But what if…" Fran started slowly. "What if Randi knew, and all the teachers only knew they had to meet at the school at a certain time and…" She snapped her fingers. "And carpool to a secret place. Which would be here. And if he's carpooling, he can't get away."

"I don't think anything good can come of it." But wouldn't it be worth it, having him in her home again, even with a bunch of other people? Just seeing him? *Look, but don't touch.* She was so over that.

"That could work." Rebekah glanced at Adriana. "I'll talk to Randi. She's been asking when I'm coming back to work, so we've been in touch."

"How long do you need to put a dinner together? Juanita will want to be involved, too," Fran put in. "We'd invite the teachers' spouses, too, right? Their families?"

"Maybe not the families. Only Lisa Brunner has kids at home." Rebekah studied Adriana. "And her kids are much older than Sam and Violet, so it wouldn't give them company."

"I don't think—"

"How long, Adriana? Two weeks? Can we do it the weekend before Valentine's Day?"

"You two are bullies."

Both women shook their heads. "We're your friends," said Rebekah.

"You need help with that stubborn man," added Fran. "You just need him in the same place as you for a few hours, and he'll come around. You'll see."

Adriana doubted it.

"Okay, so come up with a menu and let me know what I can bring. I'm good for anything you need." Fran waggled her eyebrows.

"Me, too. Plus, I'll call Randi on Monday and run it by her."

"You don't think she'll see through your ploy?"

Rebekah grinned. "There's no ploy. I'll tell her straight up."

Heat shot up Adriana's face. "No, you can't do that. You don't know what it's like to be hauled into the principal's office when you're the parent and not the child."

Rebekah shrugged. "From what I've gathered — not that you've told me everything — Randi's only objection was that Myles was Violet's teacher. You're homeschooling her now, so that's not an issue. I think she'll be on board."

Not if the principal shared Myles's aversion to homeschooling. His accusations still rankled. Not that he'd said anything she hadn't thought earlier herself. Adriana opened her mouth for further protest but shut it again. Maybe she could trust her friends. Maybe she needed to take a chance. Ignoring Myles while he ignored her certainly wasn't getting them anywhere.

"So how *is* the homeschooling coming along?" asked Fran. "Violet seems to have settled down from what I've seen at church."

"It's going better than I thought it would, partly thanks to Rebekah for some one-on-one counseling with her. It's really helped. But the best thing is that we've been reading so much together that she's starting to take off on her own."

Fran's face lit up. "I can't wait for Tieri to start reading. What is Violet into?"

"The Magic Treehouse books. Good thing the library has the whole set of them, because we're burning through them at a crazy rate. I think she likes them in particular because the little girl is just her age and loves adventures, plus she has a brother the same age as Sam who wears glasses and is a bit more cautious."

Fran grinned. "I can see her liking that. So she's reading totally on her own?"

"She is. It's so fun to see her carrying a book around.

She's even been reading to Sam. Not that he isn't perfectly capable on his own."

"That's awesome."

"It really is. I'm still reading to them both, of course. We just started on The Adventures of Huckleberry Finn, and now the kids want to raft down the river."

"Not this time of year, I hope." Rebekah shuddered. "The river is so high as snow melts in the high country."

Adriana smiled. "We'll save it for when we're at the lake this summer."

Chapter 21

A TEAM-BUILDING EXERCISE?" Myles had never been more aware of being the only male teacher in the school. Now that he intended to leave at the end of the school year — or earlier, if he could land a temp position sooner — Ms. Philson thought they should be a better team?

"Yes." The principal looked around the staff table. "I hope no one has plans for the second Friday in February. If you do, I hope this is enough notice to change them. We'll have a private dinner together and then this special training. Oh, spouses are welcome, so if you want to bring a date, Myles, go ahead."

He stared at her. Randi knew full well he wasn't dating anyone. Not with this fiasco with Adriana so fresh. Probably never again. Did she have to offer the dig in front of his colleagues? "I'd rather not, thanks."

She nodded. "It's up to you. The facilitator says the exact number of us doesn't matter. Anyone have any questions?"

Pam Novak, the sixth grade teacher, leaned forward. "Where are we going?"

Randi smiled. "That's a secret at the moment. We'll meet here at five o'clock and carpool. Is that fine with everyone?"

The teachers looked around at each other. "Works for me." Natasha shrugged.

"I think Mike has to work that evening, so I might be alone," said Pam. "I'll double check his schedule when I get home."

"We'd love to have your husband, but the main thing is if *you* can make it."

Pam nodded. "Pretty sure it won't be a problem."

"Anyone else with concerns?" Randi looked around. "If not, I'll let you go."

"Sounds fun," the kindergarten teacher, Tina, replied with a smile. "I love team-building days."

She would.

Myles didn't. The exercises were a bunch of mind games he didn't want to play. He didn't want to be a part of a team here at Bridgeview Elementary. Mentally, he had one foot out the door, as Randi knew. Was this a ploy to make him want to stay? Surely she was smarter than that.

The other teachers filed out. Myles glanced up at the principal standing at the head of the table, and she met his gaze with a smile. "I think you'll enjoy it."

He stood. "I doubt it."

Her eyebrows rose. "Your attitude is showing, Mr. Sheridan."

Myles cringed inwardly. "I'm sorry. Really, I am. I'm making every effort to keep my private life out of my work." Which he should have thought about longer in October.

"How are things going with Adriana?"

He stared at his boss. "Pardon me?"

"You're not Violet's teacher anymore."

Words burst out. "Can you believe she's homeschooling? Who even knows where she found a curriculum? I cringe to think how far behind Violet will be next year."

Randi flipped a pen end over end. "She'll make it up. Adriana told me reading has clicked with Violet. That she's reading insatiably now."

After how hard he'd worked with her for months? *Now* it clicked? Adriana would take the credit for teaching her child to read.

Myles drove his hands through his hair. He should be happy for them both. He should, but he hated being wrong. "You're not concerned about Violet being out of the school system?"

"It's just for a few months. Sam's still here, and Adriana assured me Violet will be back in the fall. If she does nothing in the intervening months but nurture a love of books, an understanding of the written word, she will be fine upon her return."

"There's more to school than reading. Sure, it's important." When teaching sixth grade, he'd seen the struggle poor readers faced in every subject. "But there's the structure. The expectations. The social aspects."

"Why are you really so upset about it, Myles?"

"I can't believe you're even asking. You're an educator. You know how vital every day of school is."

"Do you honestly think a few months out will put Violet Diaz behind for life?"

For life? "Well, maybe not forever…"

Randi studied him. "What's the problem, Myles?"

He couldn't answer that himself. Oh, he definitely believed in the school system, but his reaction was a bit over the top, especially for Mr. Non-Confrontational.

"I think you're afraid. You've played it safe all your life, you took a chance, and it backfired. Now you're bent on backtracking and preserving your hide."

"You're the one who told me to make sure it didn't spill over into work."

"And you're the one who didn't listen. But it happened, Myles. I'll agree the situation isn't ideal, but you got what you wanted — a clear path to Adriana Diaz. The only reason I can think of why you've withdrawn is fear. Unless she's turned you down?"

He clenched his mouth shut. He'd leave that last bit on the table. All of it, actually. Randi was striking far too close to home.

"Myles, I have advice for you, not that you've taken it in the past. Don't let fear hold you hostage. You've been given a gift, and you're a fool if you let it slide through your fingers."

"We found a raft!" Sam's eyes shone. "It got stuck on the river bank down by the big rock."

Adriana's kitchen bustled with women. The teachers would be arriving any minute. "I'll check it out later, but you kids stay away from the river. The water is dangerous."

"I know." Sam glared at her. "I just wanted you to know there's a raft. It's made of—"

"Stay off it. Where's your sister?" Probably trying to figure out how to float the thing down the Mississippi.

He shrugged. "Throwing a stick for Duke."

"Okay, good. Supper is in fifteen minutes, so call her to come in and wash up. And be on your—"

"Best behavior. We know, Mom."

She bumped his shoulder lightly with her fist. "Thanks." She turned back into the melee where Rebekah mashed garlic roast potatoes, Juanita sliced the leg of lamb, and Fran carried goblets of water and wine to the immaculately set table.

Adriana took a deep breath and ran sweaty hands down her gray dress pants. This evening was going to be a disaster. How could it be anything else? But she had to take the chance. For one thing, her friends wouldn't let her get out of it. For another, something had to give. She couldn't keep living like this.

Who knew the only solution left open to her — keeping Violet home — would drive an even deeper wedge between her and Myles? Men. So unpredictable. So stubborn.

The first car turned in the driveway, the second and third parking along the curb. This was it.

"Are you certain Myles is coming?" Fran peered out the kitchen window.

Rebekah glanced up. "Randi said she'd make sure of it."

He wouldn't have backed out. He had no reason to suspect anything. Randi promised to keep the destination a secret.

"Oh, there he is," Fran went on. "Getting out of the backseat of Pam's car."

Rebekah hurried over. "Yikes, he does not look happy."

Great. Adriana's heart sank.

Juanita touched her arm. "We're all praying for you, hon. God's got it."

Adriana drew in a long breath as Fran rushed to open the door. "Thanks. I'm really nervous."

"Don't be." Juanita turned to greet the incoming teachers.

Several of the spouses had come, too. Having another man or two in the mix should make Myles feel less conspicuous. Adriana smiled at her guests, shaking their hands. Tonight was not the time for the kissing of cheeks. If she tried to kiss Myles's cheek, she'd probably miss and kiss his lips instead. "So glad you could come. Please, make yourself at home." She and Fran hung coats in the closet.

Myles was the last one through the door.

"Hi, Myles."

His jaw clenched as he glanced at her then away. "Hi."

She ached to kiss him. Catch those soft lips hidden amidst his neatly trimmed beard and mustache. How could he seem so cold now when he'd exuded such love and warmth only weeks before? When she'd built up hopes and dreams of a future with him? She loved him, flaws, stubbornness, and all. Maybe she shouldn't, not when he didn't seem willing to fight for their future. She was willing, though. She had enough grit for both of them if need be. She hadn't gone this far down the path to give up easily. Not when he'd stolen her heart.

"Hi, Mr. Sheridan!" Sam appeared at his elbow, eyes bright behind smudged glasses.

"Hey there, Sam. How's it going?"

"Me'n'Violet found—"

Natasha Bertoli cleared her throat.

"Violet and I found…" Sam grinned at his teacher and turned back to Myles. "*We* found a raft stuck on the edge of the river. It's made of two logs and it's really cool."

Wasn't this section of the Spokane River considered dynamic at the best of times? Even though the river eddied out into a small bay below Adriana's property. "You know it's not safe, right?"

"I know. Mom already told us. But it's still cool. Did you know Huckleberry Finn had a raft? He used it to help free a slave. He was a hero."

Hero. Myles had never been anyone's champion. "Uh, yes, I've read that book." Eyebrows raised, Myles looked down at the eight-year-old. "Have you?"

"Mom's been reading it to me'n'Violet. I mean, Violet and me. She said it's the kids' version."

Myles wouldn't have thought of Adriana as one to focus on the classics. But why not? She wasn't a shallow person.

He still couldn't believe he'd been hoodwinked into coming to her house. By the wide smile on Randi Philson's face as she chatted with Adriana and Juanita, this had all been a setup. Did the other teachers know? Probably they'd known all along. Or possibly he was taking it too personally… yet nothing else made sense. His supervisor had certainly made it clear last week that he was foolish for not taking the opportunity to pursue Adriana. But what was he supposed to do?

Violet strutted in from the back deck, hands and jeans covered in mud.

Adriana flushed. "Off you go to get washed and changed, sweetie, and brush your hair. We're nearly ready to eat."

The little girl rolled her eyes and stomped down the hallway. Sounds of splashing water filtered to the main area followed by dresser drawers grating back and forth.

Myles's gaze caught on Adriana as she surveyed the table. She looked amazing in those gray pants and the long purple top that brushed her hips. She looked amazing in everything he'd ever seen her in.

His heart ached. Was he only being stubborn? Was he senselessly pushing away the best thing that had ever happened to him because of a little fear?

She glanced over and their eyes caught. She looked wary, and he couldn't blame her. Not after the way he'd treated her. Had he really expected her to trust him and Violet together in the classroom? How would he have dealt with it? He would have, somehow. It's what he was trained to do. But it wouldn't have been easy.

Was it was more that she thought it was okay to remove her child from school without consulting him? Not that he'd answered her emails after New Year's Eve. Yeah, it was all his fault. Everything.

Adriana broke eye contact first. "Violet and Sam made place cards for everyone, so please find your chairs."

"Oh, those are adorable!" gushed Natasha as she tugged her husband around the table to the seats reserved for them.

From the corner of his eye, Myles caught Rebekah setting plates at the kitchen island as Violet and Sam climbed onto the two tall stools. Right there was where he'd first touched Adriana. Held her in his arms. Kissed her.

Maybe he *was* a fool. Maybe he should swallow his pride mixed with that debilitating fear that he could never measure up. Adriana's father's words had only reminded him of the man he thought himself. That didn't mean he couldn't become a better man. A worthy man.

Only God could do that in him. It was a full about-face from the coward he was.

"Myles?" Juanita's hand touched his arm. "Your seat is right over there."

He blinked back to reality and accepted the seat between Pam's husband and Natasha. Directly across the table,

Adriana stood with her hands on the back of a chair. It would be a great view all through dinner. One that would weaken his resolve. Was that the plan?

"I'd like to say grace before we dig in." Adriana waited while chatter died down then closed her eyes. "Thank You, Father God, for Your many blessings. Thank You for good food, for good friends, and good teachers who care about our children. Please bless our evening together. In Jesus' name, amen."

A few murmurs of "amen" sounded from around the table. Then the platters of roasted lamb and bowls of aromatic vegetables began their passage along with several salads. It looked amazing. Smelled amazing. But how could he eat when his stomach felt like a lump of lead?

Chapter 22

"DUKE, NO!" Adriana clapped her hands to get the giant dog's attention. "I'm sorry, everyone. I'll just put him outside."

That dog. Myles stifled a grin, the first one that had tried to surface since the Bridgeview Elementary staff at descended on the Diaz house. First one in a few weeks, actually.

Duke added a dimension — literally and figuratively — to the blanket on the floor already crowded with an assortment of items. Maybe Myles should announce that the object he resonated with most was the dog, who'd looked utterly ridiculous trying to find a place to curl up on the blanket. Randi certainly hadn't left enough space for him.

But, yeah. Misfit was an apt term for Myles, too. Maybe he could still claim Duke. After all, the Great Pyrenees had been on the blanket. It should still count.

Duke ambled over to the French door to the back deck as Adriana opened it.

Adriana. Myles had been trying so hard not to notice her, but it was impossible. She had such a presence. Problem was, there was nowhere else to look. He hadn't been in her home often, but every inch exploded with memories of times they'd spent together.

"I can't believe how mild the weather's turned," Natasha said as the whisper of fresh air flowed into the room.

"I know, right?" Pam turned to face the group. "We'll be out in the school garden again in no time. My class planted tomato seeds today. Once they're up, we'll move them out to the greenhouse."

The door clicked shut, and Adriana resumed her seat in the circle.

Randi cleared her throat. "Okay, let's try this again. Rebekah, can you pass around the basket? Everyone just take out the first thing you touch, please."

Basket? But... what about the things on the blanket? Myles reached in and came out with a table knife. He turned it over. How in creation was he supposed to resonate with this?

"Now I want everyone to look at the person sitting three over on your left and think about how the item in your hand might relate to that person."

No. That's not how this activity went. How could she just make up new rules to a game he'd played at several events before? He hated surprises. Myles glanced over to see Pam's husband, Mike. He'd only met the guy a couple of times before tonight.

"I'll start." Randi peered to her left. "Adriana, this boomerang reminds me of you because no matter what happens to you, you always come back to your center. I really admire that about you." She nodded to Garry Bertoli. "Your turn. You've got Juanita."

He turned over the cross in his hands. "Easy one. I know you're the pastor's wife, so this cross fits because you're religious."

Natasha held up a bottle of perfume and leaned toward the school secretary. "Diana, this reminds me of you because your presence in BES is like a sweet fragrance. I really appreciate that about you."

Others murmured their agreement, and Diana's face flushed.

Adriana's turn. Two people sat between her and Myles. A wash of icy fear rolled over him. She had him. He was terrified to see what item she held in her hands. What she'd say about him in front of his colleagues. He tightened his grip on the knife, lest it slip from his clammy hands.

She held up a math flash card. "Myles, the easy answer would be that you taught my daughter to appreciate numbers and how they relate to each other, but I'll go one step further."

Did he dare meet her gaze? Slowly his eyes rose from the card she displayed to the brown eyes he adored.

"One thing I've noticed about you is that two plus two always equals four."

Was that a bad thing? Or a good thing? From the look on her face, he couldn't tell.

She looked down and bit her lip. "A person always knows how things stand."

What was he supposed to make of that? She wasn't even making sense. Did she want him to be wishy-washy with a new answer every five minutes? It wasn't in his nature. His heart sank, just a little. That's what she was getting at. He wasn't adaptable.

"Myles? You have Mike Novak."

He startled. Everyone was looking at him. How had he missed the two reveals in between? He held up the knife. How did it remind him of the sixth grade teacher's husband? The man was so soft-spoken it certainly wasn't for his cutting wit. "Uh, this knife reminds me of Mike because it's long and skinny, just like him."

What a dumb thing to say. A flush crept up his face. Thank the Lord for beards that hid the evidence.

The remainder of the game went by in a blur. Adriana's children passed the group and headed outside into the lingering light. From the backyard, he could hear, "Fetch, Duke!" and imagined Sam throwing a stick for the large dog.

"That was interesting, don't you think?" asked Randi brightly. "Now let's have another look at the items on the blanket on the floor. Pick something that resonates with you. This time we'll start with Diana and go counter-clockwise. Remember, more than one of you can pick the same object. That's not a problem. Diana, what object draws your attention, and why?"

Myles tuned out Diana and Juanita's responses, trying to see the blanket through Adriana's eyes. What would she pick? Probably the garden gloves. Then she'd talk about the school program she'd worked so hard to establish. That he was such a failure at teaching.

"My grandmother always had a five-year diary like that one over there. It had a little lock, and she hid the key. I always wondered what secret things she wrote in it that needed to be locked up." Adriana shook her head. "After she passed away, my sister and I helped Mom go through Grandma's things. I found the key and opened one of her stash of diaries. You know what I found?"

Heads shook around the circle.

"The weather. Who'd called. What she'd picked from the garden." Adriana gave a sardonic chuckle. "Everything was mundane. I was so disappointed. Why lock away memories like that? Memories are like the mist on the river. No longer tangible. Nothing that can be kept under lock and key. Nor should they be."

Myles's mind bounced back to that October night when they'd talked about faith. The substance of things hoped for, the evidence of things not seen... whether obscured by mist or some other way.

Had he allowed his fear to steal his faith? Had he allowed his fear to grab onto the first real obstacle in the path of love and make it a matter of pride? That table knife — it was more like him than Mike Novak. He was made of steel, unyielding, unbending. It no longer seemed like a good thing.

"Mom!" yelled Sam. Feet pounded across the deck and the door lurched open. "Mom, Duke's in the river! Violet threw a stick, and he went after it."

Fear paralyzed Adriana's body for a brief instant. A high volume of water swirled through their eddy this time of year. Duke was big, a strong swimmer with no fear of the river. But was he strong enough?

She ran out onto the deck, her gaze sweeping the water. Duke paddled valiantly not far from shore, nose into the current. Slowly the river pulled him downstream.

Violet!

Adriana's heart clogged her throat.

The little girl lay, tummy down, on a pair of logs at the

river's edge, stretching for Duke's collar, her toes digging into the bank.

"Violet!" Adriana screamed.

Myles pounded down the steps and across the long sloping yard. Before he'd passed the chicken coop, the makeshift raft pulled loose from the shore.

Violet, realizing she was adrift, looked over her shoulder with panicked eyes just as the raft caught in the edge of the current and slammed Duke in the shoulder. Raft, child, and dog vanished around the bend in the river.

Adriana bolted after Myles, vaguely aware of others running behind her. What would she do when she made it around the bend? Watch helplessly as her daughter drowned in the turbulent icy water? *No. Please, Lord, no. Protect Violet somehow. She wasn't being disobedient. She was trying to rescue her very best friend. Duke.* How would Adriana cope if only she and Sam were left behind?

She stumbled, and strong arms caught her.

"It'll be all right."

Who was that? Adriana pushed away, peering up at Mike Novak. She tore away from him, out the gate and along the river, thankful she'd insisted everyone keep their shoes on. How far ahead was Myles? She stubbed her foot on a rock. Maybe more than once, but it didn't matter. All that mattered was rescuing Violet. Rescuing Duke.

How *could* this have happened? She'd drilled safety and respect for the river into the children since they first toddled in the back yard. Only last fall had Violet become tall enough to reach the latch. She knew better than to open it. Knew the river was dangerous.

Adriana stumbled around a clump of trees just in time to see Myles jump into the water.

205

As if her heart hadn't already stopped.

She screamed, but Myles didn't turn back. The logs, with Violet gripping tightly, bobbed not far from shore, but the water was deep. Swift.

Myles's strong arms pulled him at an angle to intersect the raft.

She should help him — how? She had no idea — but something held her back. Hands on her arms. She tried to shake them off, but the grip only tightened.

"I called 9-1-1," came Randi's voice. "They're on their way."

"Is there a rope back at the house?"

Adriana stared at Mike Novak, trying to make sense of his words. "Hanging in the carport?" But was it long enough? Strong enough?

Myles. She couldn't bear to lose him, too. *Lord, please, protect him. Please, please, please give him strength.*

But how much strength would it take? How could anyone fight the river and win? The raft slammed into his chest and he went under, surfacing beside it, grabbing on. Violet flung herself at him, and they both went under, the logs floating free.

Before another scream could rend from Adriana's throat, they'd reappeared, Violet with both arms around Myles's neck, all but strangling him. He grabbed the raft, missed, surged again, and caught it.

Breathe, Adriana, breathe. As though her inhale and exhale could bring air to Myles's and Violet's lungs.

The spectacle continued to drift down the river. Adriana and the others hurried after it, rounding a clump of cottonwoods standing in the water.

Distant sirens wailed, coming closer. She hated the sound of them. Every time they rose it meant someone, somewhere was in dire need. Stephan had always perked up, even when he wasn't on duty. Always mused at what might be happening. Often reported back to her once he knew.

This time the sound was for them. For Violet. Duke. Myles.

Somehow Myles convinced Violet to swing around to straddle his back rather than cling to his throat. He grasped the raft with his strong arms, his legs kicking behind.

Maybe Adriana could breathe. Maybe they'd be okay.

The raft glanced off a towering cottonwood and bounced further into the main current.

Someone screamed.

Juanita's voice cut through the noise. "Dear Jesus, please be with Myles. Give him strength. Protect him and Violet."

The scream had been hers. Adriana's.

Chapter 23

ANOTHER WAVE OF icy water rolled over Myles. If Violet's arms weren't all but cutting off his air supply, he might have swallowed more of it. Her tight grip was welcome, though. It meant she was alive and strong. She would need that strength yet.

There could be rocks in the water. Submerged trees. And up ahead a few miles lay treacherous rapids he had no desire to run with a rickety raft and a child. Surely he could get Violet out of the river before then, but his strength was failing. Cold seeped into his bones and slowed his reflexes, muddied his thinking. His best plan was to hang onto that raft, keep angling for the near bank, and hope for the best.

And pray.

Not that he'd stopped since he plunged into the water. The repetitive plea for God's strength and wisdom spiraled in the back of his mind, barely registering in his conscious thoughts. *Nothing* registered there anymore.

Even the sound of sirens came closer then faded away. For a few minutes he'd thought help was coming, but it couldn't be. It took longer to mobilize a rescue team than that. Although he'd been in the river for what seemed like hours. Who knew how much time had passed?

"Catch this!" boomed a voice.

Myles nearly let go of the logs in his surprise. He lifted his head and tried to focus.

A whirling orange donut spun across in front of him. He felt Violet's grip change, like she was going to go for it. "Don't let go!" he yelled.

Her hands dug into his throat.

They'd cross the rope in seconds. Could he grab it? Trust it? Trust someone was at the other end, ready to haul them ashore? There were trees. Rocks. But up ahead were islands. Bridge pilings. Rapids.

Myles blinked, trying to focus on the yellow rope.

Now!

He shoved the raft and grabbed the rope, felt it slide through his numb fingers.

The word "no" screamed through his mind. He'd lost the raft. Couldn't hold the rope. He was going to die, and Violet would die with him. Adriana would—

No.

The orange lifebuoy rammed into his hands and he clutched it with desperation and all the strength he could muster. Felt the swing as the current carried him further downriver. Felt the tow as the rope held.

"Hang on! We've got you."

He clung, like Violet clung to him. Slowly — painfully slowly — their rescuer hauled them closer to the riverbank until Myles's feet hit stones and he cried out. Someone waded in and plucked Violet from his back. He could breathe again, he thought, just as he fell face first into the water.

Adriana scrambled to her daughter lying on a stretcher. A paramedic tucked a warm blanket around Violet's still form.

"Violet, sweetie. I'm here." She brushed drenched hair from her daughter's cold face.

Her daughter blinked at her. Whispered, "Mommy." Closed her eyes.

"Is she okay?"

The paramedic nodded. "Her vitals are good. It will take her a while to warm up, and I bet she'll have some bruises. We'll do a more thorough check at the hospital to make sure."

Sam crowded up beside the stretcher, tears pouring down his face.

Adriana hugged him then pivoted, searching the bank. Rescuers bent over Myles.

Myles. He'd dived straight into the turbulent, freezing water without any hesitation. His only thought had been Violet. What would they ever have done if he hadn't been there? Been so quick? The emotions of the past hour — had it been more? Less? She didn't know — rolled over her like the river had poured over the raft. Over Violet.

Over Myles.

"Here's a jacket."

Adriana blinked at the man. Mike Novak.

"I grabbed all the coats I could find and drove back. Put something on, Adriana."

She reached for her fleece jacket and peered past him. "Thanks. I need to see Myles." She staggered to the stretcher and dropped to her knees in the small space between the burly paramedics.

Someone tucked a blanket around him, covering his soaked clothing. "He's stable. Let's get him over to Deaconess."

Adriana bent and brushed his blue lips with her own. "Myles. Thank you. You're my hero. You always will be."

His eyes blinked open and his mouth tilted upward at the corners.

"No need to speak. There's time for that. I love you, Myles."

"Love you," he whispered, his gaze pinning her.

"Excuse us, ma'am. We need to load him and the girl. Are you his wife?"

If only. She shook her head. "I'm the girl's mother."

"You can ride with her. And don't worry, okay?"

"We'll follow you with Sam," Rebekah assured her.

They rolled the stretchers into the backs of two ambulances, and a paramedic helped Adriana in beside Violet. "You okay, sweetie?" Her little girl never lay this still.

"I was so s-scared, Mommy."

Adriana stroked her hair. "I know, sweetie. I was, too."

"Mr. Sheridan rescued me."

"I know. He was brave." The thought she might have lost them both threatened to overwhelm her. "So very brave."

"Is he brave like my daddy?"

Tears prickled Adriana's eyes. "Every bit as much."

"Mommy, where's Duke?"

The dog! Panic swept her. When had she last seen him? He'd disappeared down the river ahead of Myles and Violet. "There are people looking for him. I'm sure he'll be okay. He's a strong swimmer." How could she have forgotten her beloved dog even for a minute?

211

"I didn't mean to throw the stick over the fence. I forgot the gate was open from when Sam and I went to look at our raft."

"It's okay, sweetie. I know you didn't mean to." This wasn't the time to layer on guilt. Violet had had a scare she wouldn't soon forget.

"I'm sorry, Mommy."

"I know. I love you."

Myles was warm. Dry. But every muscle and inch of skin on his body throbbed in agony. He was in too much pain to be dead.

Violet.

He managed to get one eye open in the dimly lit room. Where was he? The antiseptic odor told him. Deaconess Hospital. A vague memory of sirens came back to him. Of an orange ring. Of a weight off his back.

Of Adriana's brown eyes filled with tears. Her words. "I love you, Myles." Maybe it was worth waking up and healing.

"He's awake," came a soft voice. "You can come in for a minute."

Myles tilted his face toward the sound and got both eyes open just as Adriana entered the room, an arm around the shoulder of each child.

Violet broke free and rushed toward him, climbing onto the bed before anyone could stop her. She threw her arms around him, crying. "I'm sorry I said I hated you, Mr. Sheridan. I don't hate you. You took care of me, and I'm sorry you have a broken foot."

Was that what the pain at the other end of his body was all about? He was lucky it wasn't more, considering all the rocks and trees in the water.

Myles got a hand free to rub Violet's shoulder. "It's okay, honey. I'm glad you're okay." She was, right? Otherwise she wouldn't have come running in.

Sam stood beside the bed, eyes bright behind his glasses. "That was awesome, Mr. Sheridan. You hung onto that raft even when it was bucking like a bull at the rodeo."

Violet's head popped up. "Like mutton busting?"

"Yeah!" Sam beamed. "Just like that. Our raft is pretty good, isn't it? Huckleberry Finn would've liked it."

The raft was well on its way to the Nine Mile Dam by now. Probably just as well. But if Violet had fallen into the river without the logs, she might not have fared so well.

"And those rescue guys found Duke, too."

Myles raised his eyes to Adriana's. "They did? Is he okay?"

She nodded, eyes gleaming with unshed tears. "He was drifting when they found him, all his energy gone, his nose barely above the water."

Myles knew what that felt like, but he'd had a raft to hold onto.

"He has a few cuts and scrapes, but nothing that won't heal."

Just like him, more or less. He filled his gaze with her. Why had he let his stubborn pride push her away? Life was too short not to love. Too unpredictable. He stretched his hand toward her.

Adriana cleared her throat. "Out you two go now. Juanita is waiting in the corridor."

Violet smooched him on the cheek then giggled. "That tickles."

He'd whisker-rub her some other day when he had the energy. Today — right now — he'd let her slide off the bed and dash out the door behind her brother.

Adriana knelt beside the bed and captured his hand between both of hers. "Myles, I learned something today."

She was gorgeous. Her hair, still damp, draped over one shoulder in a long braid. Her black fleece jacket was unzipped just far enough to show a turquoise shirt collar. But it was her eyes that drew him in, brown with golden flecks.

"What was that?"

"Never to let go of someone I love." She brought his hand up to her face and kissed it, her gaze never leaving his.

Her lips brought his body temperature at least one degree closer to normal right there. "I learned something, too." He slid his hand from between hers and caressed her jaw. "That pride is a downfall, for one thing. I clung to hope. Hope to bring your daughter back to you."

"You succeeded. Oh, Myl—"

He placed his finger across her lips. "I'm not done. I clung to faith. Remember that? The substance of things hoped for. The evidence of things not seen."

"I remember." Her lips caught his finger. Kissed it.

"And now abide faith, hope, and love, these three. But the greatest of these is love."

"Love never fails." Adriana leaned over the bed and placed her hands on his cheeks. "I love you, Myles."

"I love you, Adriana." He wrapped one arm around her shoulders and kissed her as well as he could lying flat on his back on a hospital bed. Which was well enough indeed.

Chapter 24

MYLES PAUSED IN THE open doorway of Randi Philson's office. "You wanted to see me?"

"Come on in and have a seat. How's the foot?"

He grimaced as he lowered himself into a chair. "Weak after so long in a cast. But physical therapy starts after school on Monday. Hopefully it won't be long before I'm back up to speed."

She leaned back. "Is swimming on your list of exercises?"

"It sure is. Long laps in the pool. I don't plan to swim in a river again for a long time, though." He shook his head. "Never again in winter."

"How's it been, having Violet Diaz back in the classroom?"

Myles's heart swelled. "Good. And I have to eat my words. Adriana did good with homeschooling her. She's

215

reading so well now." He chuckled. "I never knew she could be so cooperative, either. She hangs onto my every word and practically worships the ground I walk on. Or hobble on."

An amused grin crossed Randi's face. "A bit of hero worship, then?"

"I guess. It's a nice change."

"I imagine. So you and Adriana are still seeing each other?"

Myles reminded himself that, yes, it *was* the principal's business, being as it overlapped into the school. "We are." How much more should she know? Best to come clean. "Now that I'm rid of the cast, I plan to ask her to marry me."

"Congratulations." The smile reached her eyes. "I thought that might be coming. And it's part of the reason I invited you in today."

His breathing hitched as a knot formed in his stomach. An invitation? He'd seen it as a summons. An order. "Oh?"

She picked up a pen and began to flip it between her hands. "I assume you heard that Pam's daughter has been admitted to a drug rehabilitation center."

Myles nodded. His heart broke for Pam and Mike both. Mike, especially, had been such a support the day of the unauthorized swim and kept in touch with Myles afterward. A good man. Good people.

"Pam asked for a leave of absence to care for their grandchildren. She feels they need her undivided attention at this time."

"Understandable."

"So I need to post a substitute teaching position through to the end of the school year, and I wondered..."

Myles waited as she pursed her lips then raised her gaze to meet his. "Myles, would you like to teach sixth grade for the remainder of the term? I know that's where most of your experience lies. If you're interested, I plan to ask the board to hire Ms. Hilton to take your class. She fit in well subbing for you while you were recuperating." She held up a hand. "That's a temporary assignment for you both, unless Pam chooses not to return and you wish to make it permanent."

His head reeled. "That would be perfect." Maybe he should ask for time to pray and consult with Adriana? No. "I'd prefer to go back to the younger grades in the fall, though."

Randi grinned. "I thought you might, though it's a few years yet before Sam or Violet is in sixth."

"I'll still be in their life when they're that age." Lord willing. Now that was something he'd been praying about a lot. Him and Adriana together. "I expect to be their stepdad long before then. And it would still be better if I didn't teach them."

She nodded. "Agreed. So is a temporary transfer something I can recommend to the board?"

"Please. I heard good things from both students and parents about Ms. Hilton while I was off. I think they'll be happy to have her back for longer."

"Not at your expense, Myles. Your class loves you. You know that, right?"

He shook his head in wonder. "I know." All the cards they'd made to brighten his suite, the meals dropped by, the reports from Juanita Ramirez, Heather Sund, and others. "Part of me feels like I'm making it unnecessarily unsettling for the school. Switching will disturb two classrooms, not just Pam's."

"And the other part?"

"The other part knows it would be better to let someone

217

else teach Violet. I know Adriana is poised to homeschool again if needed, but this would allow her to relax and enjoy being a regular parent again. And she knows she won't be back on PTA to avoid a potential conflict of interest there."

"Good plan." Randi nodded. "I'll make the calls and confirm with you over the weekend. You might want to spend some time brushing up on sixth grade. Pam's class has transplanted their tomato seedlings out to the greenhouse, plus they've got other seeds sprouting. They're an eager group."

"I'm up for the gardening module. Still a lot to learn, for sure, but Adriana has been coaching me."

"That's good, because the sixth grade parents are possibly more invested in the program than the parents of the younger students. They are trying to pack everything into the children's last year at BES."

"No problem." He grinned. "And thanks, Randi. I owe you one. I never meant to cause so much trouble this year."

She rose, laughing, and stretched her hand across the desk. "Let it go, Myles. This is the best possible outcome for everyone, even Pam's daughter. I know you're a praying person. I'm sure they'd appreciate you putting in a good word to the guy upstairs for her rehabilitation."

"Definitely." Myles stood and shook his boss's hand. "Thanks for everything. I'll clean the personal items out of my desk before I head out today." He turned, his foot sending a sharp reminder that healing had not yet been completed.

"Grab a bin from the storage room, and you can put it under Diana's desk. Oh. One more thing."

"Yes?"

"You'll still have a Romero in your classroom. Hunter instead of Sky, but Catalina will continue to be an issue."

218

"Yeah, I already thought of that. I'm on her avoid-if-possible list these days, so I'm sure it will be okay. Like you say, it's only for a few months."

"Have a good weekend, Myles."

He shuffled back to his classroom, glad to be off the crutches, and looked around. The children were long gone, a few items strewn in their haste to depart. He straightened each chair, praying for that particular child as he did so. He'd miss these kids, but Randi offered a solution that was best for everyone. There'd been a lot of "Ms. Hilton this" and "Ms. Hilton that" when he'd returned to work. The students would be fine.

Myles opened his desk drawer and tucked his personal items into a bin. As he crossed to the corridor door, Violet's artwork caught his attention from the bulletin board. She'd drawn herself clinging to his back in the river. He touched the picture, feeling the nubby crayon edges.

"Thank You, Jesus."

"It was nice of Fran to invite the kids over for the afternoon." Adriana glanced over at Myles as he cycled beside her. "It seems we don't get much time without them."

At least in daylight. He came for supper most nights and stayed all evening. Sam and Violet preferred him to read the bedtime story, and they'd burned through the remainder of *The Adventures of Huckleberry Finn* and were somewhere in the Borrowers series by now. Adriana had used the extra time to hand-sew a million sequins on Eden's wedding dress.

"I think regular adult dates are important for couples." He gave her a wink.

"I think bikes are stupid."

Myles laughed. "Why do you say that?"

"Because I can't hold your hand or snuggle. I can get exercise anytime. I don't want to waste a perfectly good date keeping this much distance between us. Besides, isn't your foot still recovering? It must be hurting by now." He'd only had the cast off for a month or so.

Still chuckling, he swung his leg over his bike and hopped off while it was still rolling. The laugh cut off as he winced.

Men. Adriana hit the brakes then dismounted. She laid her bike beside his along the Centennial Trail.

"Come here, you." Myles reached for her, enveloping her in his strong arms.

This was more like it. She slid her hands around his waist and felt his solid heartbeat through his T-shirt. Smelled the masculine scent of him. Felt his lips on her hair.

Adriana tilted her head to accept his kiss. "I love you," she whispered against his lips.

He trailed kisses along her jaw and down her throat, causing a shudder to run through her.

She clutched his head as he nuzzled her neck. "Myles," she gasped.

Instead of straightening and kissing her waiting lips, he sank to one knee and rubbed his healing foot.

Had he overdone it? Should she have stopped their ride sooner? It looked like she definitely should have. But wait. Myles looked up at her as he pulled something from the pocket of his khakis then held a small velvet box toward her.

"Adriana, my sweetheart, I can't imagine life without you. I love you so much more than I ever dreamed possible. Will you marry me?"

Her heart surged. "Yes! I'll marry you tomorrow."

That smile creased his face as he slid the ring on her third finger, left hand. It had waited, unadorned, for so long. She angled her hand and watched, mesmerized, as the diamond glinted in the sunshine. It didn't matter that the gem was smaller than the one Stephan had given her. The love she had with Myles was just as large. Even more precious, in some ways, since it had been so unexpected... and so thoroughly tested.

She raised her eyes to his. "It's beautiful, Myles. I love you."

He brushed his lips across hers, awakening every nerve ending in her body. "Tomorrow's already taken. I don't think Eden and Jacob want a double wedding."

He had a point. Adriana had labored long hours over Eden's wedding gown as well as the bridesmaids dresses for Hailey and Kass. Would she design and sew her own? Only if it were a much simpler design. She didn't want to wait that long.

Her knees trembled as he kissed her again. "Vegas next weekend then."

"I want a proper wedding, sweetheart, with friends and family around us." Myles's blue eyes searched hers. "I know you've already experienced that, but I haven't, and I want to claim you as publicly as possible. I want the whole world to know how much I adore you, to witness our promises to each other. I want Violet and Sam to take part somehow."

"Really?" The idea had merit, but what man cared about the actual wedding as much as what came after it?

221

"And then I want to take you away, just the two of us, for a couple of weeks. Maybe Hawaii. Or Paris." His lips teased at hers. "I want to know you. Every part of you. I love you."

She wanted that, too. Only she wanted it now.

"And then..."

There was more?

"And then I want to pick up Violet and Sam and spend a couple of weeks at the lake like my family used to do when I was a boy. And I want to build a raft with them, and help them overcome their fear of the water."

It was true the kids hadn't been past the chicken coop since the day everything changed. "Anything else, Mr. Sheridan?"

Myles looked deeply into her eyes. "I want to kiss you until you can't stand up. Every single day, as long as we both shall live."

She caught his face between both her hands. "How about you get started now? Less talk, and more action."

Chapter 25

"GOOD RIDE?" Myles grinned at Adriana as they parked their bikes beside the carport.

She waggled the fingers on her left hand, watching the sunshine glint across the diamond. He'd caught her doing that several times on their way back to her house.

"One of the better ones, I must say." Radiance lit her face. "Will you always reward me so well for getting exercise?"

He chuckled. "Or maybe the exercise will *be* the reward."

"Oh, you." Adriana smacked his arm. "You're the one who thinks the wedding should be after school's out, so don't talk to me that way."

Seemed he ought to be embarrassed, but... why? She'd agreed to marry him — not that he'd doubted the outcome. If he'd been worried, he wouldn't have planned the extravaganza he had. He tugged her to his side and kissed her hair as they strolled toward the house. "What's for supper? Do you want me to grill burgers, maybe?" He reached for the handle and pushed the door open.

"Surprise!"

"Congratulations!"

Her parents stood just inside, flanked by his, with Violet and Sam in front of them.

"Who? What?" Adriana stepped backward onto his shoe.

Myles winced. That foot wasn't fully recovered.

"You're going to be our dad!" yelled Violet, throwing herself at him, while Sam hung back, a grin across his face.

"Welcome to the family!" Duane clapped Myles on the back.

From behind them, Stephan's parents edged closer, less exuberant, but still smiling. "Congratulations!"

Adriana pivoted, her elbow catching his gut. "How did you do this?"

"Well, there's this little device called a cell phone. You may have heard of it?"

She angled her head and narrowed her gaze.

Myles chuckled. "I've been busy. I Skyped your parents first. I know it's kind of old fashioned to ask a woman's father for her hand, but... I did that. Even though he'd given you away once before."

Tears shimmered in her eyes.

"And I looked up the Diazes as well." He nodded to Stephan's parents. It had been a bittersweet evening, that visit, but they'd offered their blessing. "It seemed like it might make for good relationships down the road. They'll always be the children's grandparents, after all."

"Thank you," she whispered.

He leaned closer, his lips grazing her ear as he whispered, "They'll take the kids when we're on our honeymoon." Myles cleared his throat. "And Fran helped me set up a party for today. I hear the best sausage in the world comes from Arcadia Valley, so your dad's on the grill."

"You went to all this trouble... for me?"

"Oh, it's no trouble, sweetheart. I don't want you to ever be sorry you said yes to me."

"I don't see how it could be possible." She wrapped both arms around his neck and kissed him thoroughly, right in front of the children, all six parents, and the crowd of friends in the background.

Once Adriana Silva. Then Adriana Diaz. Soon to be Adriana Sheridan. He liked the sound of that.

Dear Reader

Do you share my passion for locally grown real food? No, I'm not as fanatical or fixated as many of the characters I write about, but gardening, cooking, and food processing comprise a large part of my non-writing life.

Whether you're new to the concept or a long-time advocate, I invite you to my website and blog at www.valeriecomer.com to explore God's thoughts on the junction of food and faith.

Please sign up for my monthly newsletter while you're there! My gift to all subscribers is *Peppermint Kisses*, a short story set in the Farm Fresh Romance series. Joining my list is the best way to keep tabs on my food/farm life as well as contests, cover reveals, deals, and news about upcoming books. I welcome you!

Enjoy this Book?

Please leave a review at any online retailer or reader site. Letting other readers know what you think about *Memories of Mist: An Urban Farm Fresh Romance* helps them make a decision and means a lot to me. Thank you!

If you haven't read the original series, the six-book Farm Fresh Romances set on Green Acres Farm, I hope you will. The first story is *Raspberries and Vinegar*.

Keep reading for the first chapter of *Wishes on Wildflowers*, the fourth book in the Urban Farm Fresh Romances.

Wishes On Wildflowers

VALERIE COMER

GreenWords Media

Chapter One

What, Jas — *you're* going to be in charge of marketing instead? In case you've forgotten, you hate people."

Jasmine Santoro narrowed her eyes as she stared her brother down.

Basil snapped his fingers and leaned back in his chair. "I almost forgot. You also hate computers. So, I'd love to hear your marketing plans." He gave her a wide fake grin and drummed the laminate table. "Go ahead."

She surged to her feet and paced across the kitchen of the house the guys had moved into recently. The place was rundown, but the real reason they'd snapped it up was the massive backyard, perfect for the garden that would launch their new business in growing vegetables for retail. "Okay, maybe not me. But someone else."

"Jas, seriously. What's wrong with bringing Nathan Hamelin on board? He's back in Bridge-view, and he's got the creds."

She opened her mouth and closed it again. "You've got to be kidding. He'll bail out at the first sign of greener pastures elsewhere. The guy doesn't have an ounce of staying power." A fact she'd learned the hard way seven years back.

Basil rolled his eyes. "Give it up, Jas. He transferred to UCLA. That was a proactive move for his education. He wasn't abandoning Gon-zaga U."

"So it's just *me* he was abandoning?" The words spilled from her lips before she could choke them back.

"Oh, come on. You guys were kids. You expected him to give up a brilliant future and have babies with you straight out of high school?"

Jasmine raised her chin. "Other people have married their high school sweethearts and had a great marriage."

"Like who? And don't say our parents. Someone our age."

"Marco." She named their older brother.

"He was twenty-two. Still awfully young, in my opinion, but out of college." Basil shook his head. "Millennials don't get hitched until their late twenties. I don't blame Nathan for heading to California. The guy needed some air from you."

She stiffened. Why was she planning to go into business with the least favorite of her four brothers again? Right. Bridgeview Backyards was their cousin Peter's brainchild. Peter she could trust to make level-headed decisions. Only, why wasn't he here shooting down Basil's dumb idea to hire her former boyfriend? "There has to be someone else who can do a better job. Someone who's up-to-date on the Spokane vibe." Someone who wasn't Nathan Hamelin.

Anyone.

"Get over it, Jas."

Voices outside grew louder. Boots stomped on the concrete back steps. The porch door creaked open.

No. She should've been gone before now. She couldn't be caught here if that happened to be Nathan arriving with Peter. She shot a glance around the room, but the recliner Basil had inherited from Dad blocked the front door with unpacked boxes stacked around it. Besides, her boots and coat were in the entry.

Basil leaned back in his chair and crossed his arms, chuckling. It had to be Nathan in the porch, kicking off his boots, clanging the hangers.

Jasmine pointed at her big brother. "I don't even like you," she growled.

He shrugged, and the door opened. Two men entered. Peter... and Nathan.

Her heart stuttered. This Nathan had matured, at least in looks. He'd filled out some — but not too much — looking self-assured in jeans and a light gray Henley. His blond hair was shorter than it used to be, and a trimmed beard softened his square jaw. His blue eyes collided with hers. Wariness seeped out.

She straightened to her full height, a solid eight inches shorter than his six feet, and managed to keep her arms from crossing protectively over her chest. "Nathan. What a surprise."

"Jasmine." His gaze ran the length of her before meeting her eyes once again. "You look good."

Right. In her old jeans and a plaid shirt. If she'd known she'd be seeing him, she'd have dabbed on some makeup and worn that new — no. She'd have smeared dirt on her face and worn baggy sweats. That's what. His opinion of her didn't matter... though it might be fun to see regret on his face.

That would never happen. He'd had a new girlfriend in L.A. within a week of leaving Spokane. There hadn't even been a backward glance to what he'd left behind.

Peter shifted from one foot to the other, his gaze flicking between them. "Hey, Jas. Didn't expect to see you here."

Really? She forced a smile to her face. "That seems obvious. I popped by to drop off a new supply of herbal tea, but don't worry. I was just leaving."

"No need to rush away." Peter took a step closer. "Let me put on a pot of coffee, and we can talk."

"I'm not sure there's anything to discuss." Jasmine eyed the path to the door, but she'd have to brush past Nathan to get there. So not happening.

"I just told her Hamelin's joining the team." Basil slung his arm over the back of the vacant chair beside him. "She seems to be hung up on ancient history."

A fierce spurt of red shot through Jasmine's vision, and she clenched her fists against her thighs. If only she could smack that smirk off her brother's face, but she wouldn't give Nathan the satisfaction of seeing how much effect he still had over her. She breathed in and out to a count of five — twice, for good measure — and willed down the impulse. "Thanks, Basil. You're the best brother a girl could ever want." Too bad sarcasm leaked out with every word.

Basil tipped his head in acknowledgment, his grin widening.

Did her brother seriously live to tick her off? Was that his primary goal in life? And why hadn't she run for the door already?

Awkward silence surrounded Nathan Hamelin as he stood in the doorway of his friends' rental. Jasmine. She looked amazing, her long dark hair pulled into a low ponytail. She'd always looked great, no matter what she wore, but faded jeans and a plaid flannel shirt open over a black fitted T-shirt reminded him she'd never cared what others thought and looked fabulous anyway. She was all Jasmine.

Man, he'd been an idiot to bolt out of her life back then. They'd been an item for a couple of years, but her talk of weddings and babies terrified him. No way had he been ready to settle down. Not by a long shot. But instead of explaining his feelings to her and trying to slow the relationship, he'd run.

Hadn't helped comparing the thick-as-thieves Santoro clan to the sparse and barely connected Hamelins. How did someone get any privacy with practically all their family living within a few blocks of each other and in each other's business every day? And Marietta, Jasmine's grandmother, ruled the roost. He'd been terrified of the outspoken Italian woman.

Now he was only terrified of Jasmine, but somehow his gaze had tangled up with hers. He took a step backward, his hand groping for the doorknob. "I, uh, I don't need to be here."

Peter and Basil exchanged a glance. "I think you probably do," said Basil.

Peter plucked a key ring off the kitchen counter. "I can show you the basement suite now."

"Pardon me?" Jasmine stepped closer, fists settling on

her hips. "What did you say?"

Peter chewed on his lip. "Uh, Nathan might sublet the lower level from us, but he needs to see it first."

"Of course." Jasmine shot a fiery glance at Nathan. "Renting from you makes all kinds of perfect sense, since he'll be working for you and all."

"Yeah, that's what we thought." Peter's shoulders relaxed.

Premature, Santoro. Didn't you hear the tone?

"And you two didn't think to run this by me?" She pinned her cousin then her brother with her gaze. "I suppose Alex knew, and no one thought I should get a chance to voice my opinion? Which is a bit unfair, don't you think? None of the rest of you *dated* him."

Nathan winced. She was certainly voicing her viewpoint now. Not that he didn't deserve her wrath, but he'd hoped time would have helped her see how wrong they'd been for each other.

"I-I'm sorry?" Peter's gaze ricocheted between them. "You were on that essential oil retreat at Green Acres Farm when Basil brought up hiring Nathan. He said your relationship was water under the bridge."

Basil spread his hands. "It's been years. I thought it would be."

Nathan had thought so, too. Oh, he couldn't deny the mixed feelings that had stampeded through him when he'd seen the Santoro surname on her Facebook profile. Searching Jasmine out had only been idle curiosity, and her 'about' page had been sparse with her updates and photos locked down to friends-only, so he couldn't find out more. She'd have moved on long ago. He had, after all. There'd been Kendra and Pauline and then Rae, whom he'd thought might actually be The One before he'd discovered her addiction to gambling in hopes of covering her mounting credit card debt.

"I *am* over Nathan." She spit out the words.

Basil snickered.

"I just didn't think this was how we were going to run our business. I know I'm not slated to come on board full-time for another two years, but now I'm not sure I want to. Ever." She started for the door. "Excuse me, please."

Nathan shifted out of her way, but Peter stepped into it. "You're quitting because Basil hired Nathan? Look, we should have talked it through with you and Alex, but we didn't. I'm sorry. Really. Can we talk about this?"

Alex. Jasmine's younger brother was a CPA working for a big firm downtown, at least according to Facebook. Nathan remembered him as a scrawny teen who'd hero-worshiped his sister's boyfriend. Nathan had kind of liked that. Which meant Alex would be just as happy as Jasmine to see him back in Bridgeview. Great.

"No, doofus. I'm not quitting because of *him*." She shot Nathan a scowl. "I'm out because we were supposed to be a team, and teams don't make decisions without discussion." This time Basil received the brunt of her glare. "And because my big brother thinks it's hilarious to hide things from me and mock me. I can't trust him as a business partner."

Basil rolled his eyes. "Oh, give it up, Jas. So I screwed up. Sorry. It won't happen again." The sardonic grin lessened marginally.

Jasmine shook her head, her ponytail swinging from side to side. "I'm leaving now. I'll talk to you guys later. Some of you, anyway." She sidestepped Peter and pinned Nathan with a glare, jerking her thumb sideways. "Excuse me, please."

He shifted out of her way as she strode past, the whiff of

237

something sweet yet woodsy wafting over him. She smelled so... Jasmine. A minute later the porch door all but slammed shut. Then silence.

"Man, that didn't go over well." Peter grimaced. "I should have trusted my instincts and found time to consult with her about this."

"Why?" Basil stretched his long legs under the table and crossed his ankles. "It was so much more fun this way."

Why had Nathan considered Jasmine's older brother one of his keeper friends again? He'd known there was little love lost between that pair of siblings, which had seemed a good thing until now, or at least an okay thing. But Jasmine didn't deserve to be treated like this. "I'll find a different rental." Where? Moving in with his dad, even temporarily, wasn't an option. Nathan shoved the thought aside. "I'll find plenty of work in freelance marketing, so don't worry about me. I'll be fine."

Peter shook his head. "Splitting the rent one more way will make a big difference to our cash flow this first season. And we need someone experienced to help us figure out how to keep our numbers, not only in the black, but growing. Alex is doing our books. He's given us our homework, but we need help with a plan to meet his projections."

"Well, I say having Hamelin on board is more important than my sister." Basil pulled to his feet. "We can get honey from any number of sources, and her herbs and stuff are no big deal. Anyone can grow them."

Oh, boy. Good thing Jasmine couldn't hear, or those glares would turn into fireworks worthy of the Fourth of July.

Peter shook his head, his mouth tight, as he tossed the keys from one hand to the other. "First things first. Let me show you the suite, Hamelin. We'll give it a day or two and figure out what to do next."

It wasn't like Nathan had any other options for a place to sleep. Not tonight, anyway, but he'd better start looking. Being on the wrong side of Jasmine meant being on the wrong side of her grandmother, and that meant Bridgeview would be a mighty uncomfortable place to live.

Just what he needed.

Wishes on Wildflowers

is available where you purchased

Butterflies on Breezes

www.valeriecomer.com/wishes

Author Biography

Valerie Comer lives where food meets faith in her real life, her fiction, and on her blog and website. She and her husband of over 35 years farm, garden, and keep bees on a small farm in Western Canada, where they grow and preserve much of their own food.

Valerie has always been interested in real food from scratch, but her conviction has increased dramatically since God blessed her with three delightful granddaughters. In this world of rampant disease and pollution, she is compelled to do what she can to make these little girls' lives the best she can. She helps supply healthy food — local food, organic food, seasonal food — to grow strong bodies and minds.

Valerie is a USA Today bestselling author and a two-time Word Award winner. She has been called "a stellar storyteller" as she injects experience laced with humor into her green clean romances.

To find out more, visit her website at www.valeriecomer.com, where you can read her blog, explore her many links, and sign up for her email newsletter to download the free short story: *Peppermint Kisses: A (short) Farm Fresh Romance 2.5*. You can also use this QR code to access the newsletter sign-up.

www.valeriecomer.com